The Mystery of Love & Sex

Bathsheba Doran

A SAMUEL FRENCH ACTING EDITION

SAMUEL FRENCH

FOUNDED 1830

SAMUELFRENCH.COM
SAMUELFRENCH-LONDON.CO.UK

FOR PRODUCTION ENQUIRIES

UNITED STATES AND CANADA
Info@SamuelFrench.com
1-866-598-8449

UNITED KINGDOM AND EUROPE
Plays@SamuelFrench-London.co.uk
020-7255-4302

Each title is subject to availability from Samuel French, depending upon country of performance. Please be aware that *THE MYSTERY OF LOVE & SEX* may not be licensed by Samuel French in your territory. Professional and amateur producers should contact the nearest Samuel French office or licensing partner to verify availability.

MUSIC USE NOTE

Licensees are solely responsible for obtaining formal written permission from copyright owners to use copyrighted music in the performance of this play and are strongly cautioned to do so. If no such permission is obtained by the licensee, then the licensee must use only original music that the licensee owns and controls. Licensees are solely responsible and liable for all music clearances and shall indemnify the copyright owners of the play(s) and their licensing agent, Samuel French, against any costs, expenses, losses and liabilities arising from the use of music by licensees. Please contact the appropriate music licensing authority in your territory for the rights to any incidental music.

IMPORTANT BILLING AND CREDIT REQUIREMENTS

If you have obtained performance rights to this title, please refer to your licensing agreement for important billing and credit requirements.

THE MYSTERY OF LOVE & SEX was first produced by Lincoln Center Theater (André Bishop, Producing Artistic Director; Adam Siegel, Managing Director) at the Mitzi E. Newhouse Theater in New York City on March 2, 2015. The performance was directed by Sam Gold, with sets by Andrew Lieberman, costumes by Kaye Voyce, lights by Jane Cox, and sound by Daniel Kluger. The Production Stage Manager was Janet Takami. The cast was as follows:

CHARLOTTE	Gayle Rankin
JONNY	Mamoudou Athie
HOWARD	Tony Shaloub
LUCINDA	Diane Lane
HOWARD'S FATHER	Bernie Passeltiner

CHARACTERS

CHARLOTTE

JONNY

HOWARD

LUCINDA

HOWARD'S FATHER

SETTING

The play takes place on the outskirts of major cities
in the American South.

TIME

Act One takes place five years before Act Two.

ACKNOWLEDGEMENTS

I would like to thank the following people for their support and aid
in the development of this script: Mamoudou Athie, André Bishop,
Adam Greenfield, Jordan Harrison, Amy Herzog, Diane Lane, Charles
Parnell, Gayle Rankin, Ana Reeder, Tony Shaloub, Lucy Smith, Mark
Subias, Daniel Swee, Ben Whine and in particular, Sam Gold for his
incomparable dramaturgical insight and kindness, brilliance and
funniness in rehearsal, and my wife, Katie Doran, without whom this
play would not have been written.

For Ben

ACT ONE

Scene One

(Evening. An uninspiring dorm room to which **CHARLOTTE** *and* **JONNY** *have tried to add inspiration.)*

*(***CHARLOTTE, JONNY, LUCINDA** *and* **HOWARD** *stand near a very low table set for dinner. The room feels too small. Everyone is trying.)*

LUCINDA. Oh my god, it's so cute, it's so *cute*, the way you've done this.

HOWARD. What did you do? You pushed the two tables together?

CHARLOTTE. Right, we pushed the two tables together, the other one's from Jonny's dorm room, and we made one big table, like a dining room table.

HOWARD. Right.

CHARLOTTE. And we covered it with a sheet.

JONNY. I said get a tablecloth.

CHARLOTTE. We put the sheet over the table, thus transforming it into a tablecloth.

JONNY. A sheet on a table is not a tablecloth. Especially when it's flannel.

LUCINDA. I like it, it's Bohemian, isn't that what you were going for? And I love the candles. Are they scented?

JONNY. Yes they are. I got them on discount.

LUCINDA. Vanilla?

JONNY. I think maybe it was papaya? I can check, the container's in the trash.

CHARLOTTE. Honey, it doesn't matter, it's just an "ah" scent, right? Vanill-ah. Papaya-ah. Just *(She inhales and exhales luxuriously.)* Aaaah.

> *(Everyone looks at her.)*

I just mean, just like, there's no reason to involve the trash. Let's have wine.

> (**JONNY** *grabs a bottle.*)

JONNY. Yes. Who wants wine?

CHARLOTTE. We call it the Spanish red. I don't know what its real name is, but we call it the Spanish red.

JONNY. It's Tusca di Torro.

HOWARD. *(theatrically)* Ah! Di Torro!

> *(beat)*

JONNY. Exactly.

CHARLOTTE. It's very cheap but it's the *best* of the cheap. That's what I said the first time I went into the liquor store here. I said, "I want your very best cheap wine."

HOWARD. *(to* **JONNY***)* Shall I open it?

JONNY. Great.

> *(He hands the wine to* **HOWARD.***)*

And we have wine glasses.

> *(As he goes to get glasses, he and* **CHARLOTTE** *pass each other, squeezing past in the limited space.)*

Sorry, dear.

CHARLOTTE. Excuse me, angel.

> (**JONNY** *hands a glass to each parent.*)

HOWARD. And we'll need a corkscrew.

CHARLOTTE. *(to* **JONNY***)* Shall I sit down? Are you going to serve?

> *(A beat as* **JONNY** *assesses the most effective way to host a dinner party.)*

JONNY. You can sit.

(**CHARLOTTE** *sits on the floor by the table, cross-legged.* **HOWARD** *is disconcerted.*)

HOWARD. Are we sitting on the floor?

CHARLOTTE. Yes. Next to the table with the tablecloth. You didn't see that coming?

LUCINDA. I told you! Bohemian.

CHARLOTTE. Stop saying that.

LUCINDA. Sorry.

(**LUCINDA** *sits.*)

Can we smoke in here?

JONNY. It's not that Bohemian.

HOWARD. She's quitting anyway, aren't you, Lula?

LUCINDA. I have seen several hypnotists. To no avail.

HOWARD. You have to want to.

LUCINDA. I don't want to. You want me to. That must be the problem.

JONNY. You know, if everyone sits, I can serve.

HOWARD. It's just my back...

LUCINDA. I expect it's good for you to sit on a nice hard surface.

CHARLOTTE. Come on, Dad, it's supposed to be fun. It's... (*Confidence in the evening drains out of her.*) We, don't have a proper table and chairs...

HOWARD. You have chairs.

(**HOWARD** *points to a chair.*)

CHARLOTTE. I know, but then we have to put food on our laps, and I thought well this is how the Japanese do it, right? So I thought –

JONNY. I said we should eat with our plates on our laps. We still can.

CHARLOTTE. Yeah. Oh course. Let's eat with plates on our laps like old women in front of the TV. Great.

(*She stands up, knocking the table a little. A beat.*)

HOWARD. No. If this is how the Japanese do it.

(**HOWARD** *sits down next to the table.* **CHARLOTTE** *sits down next to him.*)

HOWARD. Yes, I suppose this makes sense.

(**JONNY** *brings over an enormous bowl of salad. Then he sits down. They are all round the table. Pause.*)

JONNY. Help yourself, Lucinda.

LUCINDA. This looks like the Garden of Eden and I can't wait to eat it.

(**LUCINDA** *serves herself salad.*)

CHARLOTTE. It's all fresh vegetables. We have this thing, when we're giving a dinner party, because like some people try to pretend that they have actual ovens, like we have at home, but we don't here. The dorm kitchens have this weird little machine – what's it called, Jonny?

JONNY. It's a Foreman Grill.

LUCINDA. Oh!

(*Everyone looks at her.*)

(*on the brink of laughter*) I was going to say "Bohemian" again but I didn't. I stopped myself.

(*beat*)

CHARLOTTE. Anyway, you can't really cook on it and have the food taste good –

JONNY. It doesn't *heat* anything properly.

CHARLOTTE. But some people because they're trying to be grown-ups and pretend like they have a real kitchen, which is ridiculous –

JONNY. It is. It is ridiculous.

CHARLOTTE. They cook on it. But we have this thing that we *acknowledge* the limited resources. But then work with them. So I was like…*what if we forget the heat?*

JONNY. Exactly.

CHARLOTTE. What is food without *heat?* What would that *be?*

HOWARD. *(grimly)* Salad.

CHARLOTTE. Right.

HOWARD. Just salad?

CHARLOTTE. And bread and butter.

HOWARD. Aha!

CHARLOTTE. Except no butter. I forgot to get it.

HOWARD. Just salad, honey?

JONNY. I tried to pick out hefty vegetables.

> *(Silence for a while as the salad finishes making the rounds and begins to be chewed.)*

LUCINDA. That is a piquant dressing.

CHARLOTTE. Not too much lemon?

LUCINDA. Perfect.

HOWARD. And you squeezed the lemons yourself.

CHARLOTTE. Yes. How did you know?

HOWARD. Here's a seed.

> *(He removes it from his mouth.)*

LUCINDA. Why are you being such an asshole?

HOWARD. Hey!

LUCINDA. These kids went to a lot of trouble.

HOWARD. They did?

LUCINDA. Yes!

CHARLOTTE. *(at the same time)* Yes! Jonny, can you please explain the vision behind this meal? We put a lot of thought into it actually.

JONNY. Well…there are some families for whom this is a delicious, evening meal. Salad and bread. Fresh. Simple. Natural Cuisine. It's very French. That's why we got French bread, see.

> (**HOWARD** *takes a piece.*)

HOWARD. Yes, the French love it. They do. Du pain.

> *(He takes a bite of his bread. Chews. Swallows. Everyone relaxes.)*

HOWARD. You know what else they love? Du Beurre.

    (Everyone tenses.)

(cheerfully) But you know who *don't* care about butter? The Japanese. So in a way this all makes sense.

    (He kisses his daughter on the cheek.)

Love you, honey. I'm sorry. I just miss you a lot. Driving here…oh, every mile between us was an agony.

LUCINDA. Oh your father outdid himself. Not one speeding ticket. Two.

HOWARD. I explained I was on my way to see my daughter at college who I miss more than life itself. Did they care?

LUCINDA. He explained this to both sets of highway patrol.

HOWARD. I told them, I said my little girl's going to be President of the United States some day and when she is she will hunt you down.

LUCINDA. I begged him to let me do the talking –

HOWARD. Lula, honey –

LUCINDA. You called one of the officers "sir."

HOWARD. I was being polite.

LUCINDA. It was a ma'am. That was your first mistake.

HOWARD. That was not a woman. Maybe it wasn't a man, but it wasn't a woman. Not with those sideburns.

LUCINDA. Honey, I have told you. The minute you open your mouth we have a problem. They hear you weren't born here, a Southern cop is a Southern cop, that makes them hate you. So then they want to see your license. And that is the nail in the coffin, my friend.

JONNY. What's wrong with his license?

HOWARD. Nothing at all.

LUCINDA. It's his last name. Combine it with his face and his accent and what you have is a New York Jew.

HOWARD. So I shouldn't speak?

LUCINDA. Not to highway patrol men. You should let me speak. Fact is my father's name still opens up a lot of doors in this state.

HOWARD. There was a time you wouldn't walk through a door if your father's name opened it.

LUCINDA. I am quite sure I could have gotten Madam Sideburns to relent with or without my daddy's name. But Charlotte, if you really are serious about becoming a politician and running in Georgia then you need to use my last name, not your father's.

HOWARD. I agree with her about that, honey. It will make things easier. Unless you move to New York. Then by all means, go Jew.

CHARLOTTE. I think you're underestimating the South, but whatever.

HOWARD. Listen there's nothing wrong with changing a name to get ahead. Jews have been doing it for centuries. It's the only way. That is the great advantage Jews have over black people, right Jonny. We can pass. Sometimes we get to pass.

JONNY. Right, and not being brought to America on slave ships in chains from Africa. That was also an advantage.

HOWARD. Absolutely. *(He chews his bread.)* Although there were ships. That we got on, following pogroms. Following death camps. You know what? From now on I am always going to eat bread dry. As a writer it's useful for me to identify with...everyone. Everyone. And this is definitely giving me an insight into what it might be like to be a homeless person.

JONNY. *(standing, accidentally knocking the table)* I'll go get some butter.

LUCINDA. What about some olive oil? We can dip the bread in olive oil. Like Italians.

HOWARD. This is such a cosmopolitan meal. It's almost overwhelming.

JONNY. We're actually out of olive oil. But I'll go get butter. I don't mind.

CHARLOTTE. *(standing, also accidentally knocking the table)* No, I will. I'm the one who forgot it. Even though you wrote it down. On the list.

LUCINDA. I will go and purchase butter.

HOWARD. She means go smoke a cigarette. I am not a writer of detective fiction for nothing.

CHARLOTTE. Mom, no cigarettes.

HOWARD. *(to LUCINDA)* Do the thing the hypnotist told you to do. *(explaining)* Whenever she wants to smoke she has to…

> *(He looks at LUCINDA. Do it. LUCINDA gives an exasperated sigh. Then she clicks her fingers and inhales very deeply.)*

I'm really proud of you, Lula-belle.

LUCINDA. I'm putting myself through this for you. Make no mistake about that.

> *(HOWARD kisses her. During his kiss she makes the decision to kiss him back. This all takes a few seconds. During this, CHARLOTTE indicates to JONNY that the kissing is unfortunate but beyond her control.)*

JONNY. *(to CHARLOTTE)* I'll get butter. You visit with your parents. They're here to see you.

CHARLOTTE. OK. Do you have money, angel?

JONNY. Back in a sec.

> *(JONNY exits.)*

LUCINDA. His mom has a care package for him. Remind me. It's in the car.

CHARLOTTE. Dad, can we not do the Jew versus Black thing.

HOWARD. What Jew versus Black thing?

CHARLOTTE. You know. Who had it worse?

LUCINDA. Agreed, that is a bad topic.

HOWARD. *(baffled)* That is a topic I neither raised nor discussed.

*(CHARLOTTE is about to disagree but – without
HOWARD seeing – LUCINDA indicates she should
leave it alone.)*

HOWARD. *(with cheer)* Hey! I have something for you!

(He holds out a scrap of paper.)

CHARLOTTE. What is that?

LUCINDA. Oh Jesus…

HOWARD. This is the cell phone number of one Scott Harris.
You may have heard of him. He has won an Emmy. And
stars as the brooding bastard son of Detective Grayson
in the slightly dubious TV adaptation of my books. He
wants to meet you.

CHARLOTTE. Why?

HOWARD. I may have shown him your picture.

CHARLOTTE. Why would I want to meet him?

HOWARD. He's a movie star! Regular people can't get his
number. Here is his number. Take it. *(He pushes the scrap
of paper into her hand.)* Just think about it. He's special.

LUCINDA. That's a tiny little bed they have you sleeping on
here. Has it seen much action?

HOWARD. Lucinda!

CHARLOTTE. *(at the same time)* Mom!

LUCINDA. *(to HOWARD)* I am trying to find out in a subtle
way.

CHARLOTTE. Nothing subtle is happening here.

HOWARD. *(to LUCINDA)* I think it's best to be direct. Like
this. *(to CHARLOTTE)* Are you and Jonny together now?

CHARLOTTE. *(beat)* Why do you want to know?

LUCINDA. We're curious, honey. The two of you seem…
closer…than usual.

HOWARD. I mean, you don't have to tell us, of course. But
we don't like secrets. And the two of you appear to
have all but set up house so… I'm a fan of clarity, is all.

(Suddenly, the atmosphere is serious.)

CHARLOTTE. We are not dating. Not…like…officially. I mean…like…

HOWARD. Enough with the "like." Why can't you kids ever just say what is happening? Why is there always this approximation? What *is* it? On its own terms?

CHARLOTTE. I don't know what it is! We've known each other since we were nine. We are very much beyond "dating." In the conventional sense. But…yeah, I mean it's serious. We're serious. I can't live without him. That kind of thing.

HOWARD. Jonny's mom said something about the two of you moving in together.

CHARLOTTE. We're definitely moving in together after we graduate. He's coming to D.C. with me.

HOWARD. To do what?

CHARLOTTE. A master's at Georgetown.

HOWARD. He won't get into Georgetown.

CHARLOTTE. What do you know about his grades?

HOWARD. I remember what they were in high school.

CHARLOTTE. He's very smart.

(**HOWARD** *sighs heavily.*)

Oh, don't do the sigh, Dad.

HOWARD. I think we should discuss this. In more detail. Later.

CHARLOTTE. Why? I *love* Jonny. You know that. You guys do too! He practically grew up in our house.

HOWARD. The whole point of college is to experiment. What's that song? *(loudly)* From *Bee!* To *Bee!* To *Bee!*

LUCINDA. Is he drunk?

HOWARD. It's from *The King and I.* You've got to cross-pollinate and explore your options. There are a lot of men out there. In the blink of an eye, you'll be married. Don't make a mistake.

LUCINDA. What the hell is that, the voice of experience?

CHARLOTTE. You took against Jonny because of the egg whites.

HOWARD. No, but I'll tell you what. The egg whites was a character detail that said *everything*. I write characters, that is what I do, and if I wrote a character that only ate the yolk of a boiled egg and not the outside I would intend the reader to draw conclusions from that. Because it implies taking the easy road.

CHARLOTTE. *(through gritted teeth)* It *implies* he doesn't like egg whites.

HOWARD. Who care's if he likes them! It was a meal we cooked for him and it was impolite! It was indicative of character, Charlotte! As is a straight C student in high school who did not participate in a single after-school activity –

CHARLOTTE. That's not him, that's how he was *raised*. He wasn't pushed. His mother –

HOWARD. Jonny's mother does not approve of this. She is a committed Baptist, Charlotte. She doesn't want a Jewish daughter-in-law, I don't care how sweet she is to you. And on the subject of the boy's mother –

LUCINDA. FYI the boy is out buying butter and could be back any moment.

CHARLOTTE. Is this because he's black?

HOWARD. *What?*

LUCINDA. She went there. As I told you she would.

HOWARD. Wow.

CHARLOTTE. The boy. That's racist.

HOWARD. That is *Southern* for any underling, the underling in this case being a kid a generation or three below me, who did not come home for Christmas break despite –

CHARLOTTE. He did an exchange with a school in *Finland*. It was a big opportunity –

HOWARD. There are no opportunities in Finland.

CHARLOTTE. That is so American-centric.

HOWARD. He did not come home for Christmas although it might have been his mother's last Christmas.

CHARLOTTE. She's not dying! Jonny says she's doing really well.

HOWARD. She lies to him and he chooses to believe her lies. That is an indication of character. Believe me, she's dying. A man would come home and help her get her damn groceries from the car to the kitchen and spend some time saying goodbye. Believe me. I know. ~~I did it.~~

LUCINDA. You were forty years old, Howard. Jonny's not even twenty-one. He *is* a boy. They're both just children and this is getting way too serious.

> *(She does her hypnosis cigarette thing again. Father and daughter watch for a second then:)*

CHARLOTTE. Jonny says his mother is not dying. And I think he would know better than you. *(beat)* You like Jonny, don't you Mom?

LUCINDA. *(non-committal)* Jonny's a cutie-pie.

CHARLOTTE. You and Dad met in college.

LUCINDA. That's true. A little too young. I never finished my degree and we alienated both of our families but apart from that yes, we are the perfect model.

HOWARD. You admitted in the car she could do better.

LUCINDA. Uh huh, I did. And I also told you they've been in love since they were children.

CHARLOTTE. That's what a marriage is, right? Best friends?

HOWARD. So we are talking about marriage?

CHARLOTTE. That was theoretical. *(beat)* Jonny would die if he knew we were talking like this. And he'll be back any second.

> *(**CHARLOTTE** pours herself more wine.)*

LUCINDA. I agree. Enough.

CHARLOTTE. Jonny's mom didn't do a *thing* to help him with his studies. She wouldn't pick him up for after school activities.

HOWARD. A bright kid finds a way.

CHARLOTTE. He made it here, didn't he? He's getting a degree.

(**HOWARD** *gives an ominous sigh.*)

CHARLOTTE. *(emphatically)* Let us shelve this. He'll be back soon.

HOWARD. You threw away Yale for this guy.

CHARLOTTE. I threw it away because I have never met a single person who went to Yale that is not an asshole.

HOWARD. I went to Yale.

LUCINDA. So did I. It was an asshole factory.

HOWARD. Okay, but can I go back to what I was saying? Forget Yale. Yale wasn't right. I understand that you are someone who needs to feel safe. But when we packed up your bags you were supposed to be going out into the world, not playing house in a room with a kid from back home.

(**JONNY** *enters.* **HOWARD** *does not skip a beat.*)

So I said to my publisher, "Listen, I am not beholden to you or the American public to continue writing Detective Grayson. Twenty-seven novels are enough. I'm working on something new." Hi, Jonny!

JONNY. I have butter! And also some smoked turkey.

HOWARD. Now you're talking! Hand it over.

(**JONNY** *hands it to* **HOWARD**.)

CHARLOTTE. *(to* **JONNY**) I thought we don't do processed meat.

JONNY. I think your dad wanted some more food.

HOWARD. How'd you guess, Jonny?

JONNY. I just sensed it.

HOWARD. *(making himself a turkey sandwich)* Now if only we had some Swiss cheese…you guys don't have any Swiss cheese, lying around do you?

(**CHARLOTTE** *and* **JONNY** *shake their heads.*)

No matter.

(*He makes himself a sandwich with gusto.*)

Mayo?

LUCINDA. Shut up!

JONNY. So listen, Howard. There was a favor I wanted to ask you.

HOWARD. If you go get me some Swiss cheese, the answer is definitely yes.

(**JONNY** *half-rises, uncertainly.*)

CHARLOTTE. (*firmly*) He's kidding.

(**JONNY** *sits down again.*)

LUCINDA. What is it, honey?

JONNY. I have to write a final paper this year for English Lit. And I'd like to do it on you. On your work.

LUCINDA. That is so sweet.

CHARLOTTE. I told him you'd be fine with it.

JONNY. It's a big paper. Like, the whole semester's grade basically depends on this paper. And I'm applying to graduate schools for English Lit. so like…it's really important I get a good grade. And I was thinking about Hitchcock. Like, nobody really noticed Hitchcock was a genius. Like, everyone saw his movies. But it wasn't until Truffaut that people understood that Hitchcock wasn't just an entertainer. He was an auteur.

CHARLOTTE. There's a series of interviews Truffaut did with Hitchcock –

HOWARD. Yes, thank you, I understand. I too have been to university.

LUCINDA. You want to interview Howard? Is that what you're saying, honey?

JONNY. Yes. If it's okay. Over spring break.

CHARLOTTE. The last paper he wrote he entered into a student competition, judged by the faculty. He won. Meaning it got, you know, an A. *Plus.*

(**JONNY** *is confused, although not displeased, as to why they are discussing his grades.*)

HOWARD. That is great. Did you tell your mother?

JONNY. No, it just happened.

HOWARD. I'll tell you what. You can interview me over spring break. Take as much time as you need. One condition. You go call your mother right now and tell her about your great success.

JONNY. Well…we're eating dinner, right now.

HOWARD. Your mom is having a tough time, right now. She says she only speaks to you once a week.

LUCINDA. Honey, I think you added the "only."

JONNY. I call her on Sundays when she gets back from church.

HOWARD. She's been too sick to go to church recently. Did she mention that? I know that because I bring her fresh fruit from our tree every week. You want to know the truth, you need to ask the right questions.

LUCINDA. That's a line from one of your books.

HOWARD. *(irritated)* No, it's a line that came out of my mouth right now.

LUCINDA. *(trying to lighten the mood)* I think it's in one of his books.

> *(beat)*

JONNY. So I'll call her.

> *(JONNY exits.)*

HOWARD. If he's a contender for son-in-law I will knock him into shape. Butter, please.

> *(beat)*

LUCINDA. Look, honey. Grandpa died.

> *(CHARLOTTE stares at her.)*

CHARLOTTE. Are you okay?

LUCINDA. I'm fine, sugar. A little sad. But we hadn't spoken for years, so.

CHARLOTTE. Yeah. *(beat)* I mean I don't feel anything really. I only met him a few times. Sorry.

LUCINDA. You don't need to be sorry for not feeling anything. I don't feel anything.

HOWARD. That's not true. Your mother felt a lot. Day of. Didn't you, honey? It's okay to say that.

> (LUCINDA *does her giving-up-smoking-inhalation. She tries to smile through it.*)

(to CHARLOTTE*)* I'm sorry we gave you such a lousy lot of grandparents. honey.

LUCINDA. *(sharply)* You adore your father, Howard.

HOWARD. My father is a giant pain in the ass.

LUCINDA. You think everyone is a giant pain in the ass.

HOWARD. I know, I know. The two of you are really the only people I can tolerate.

CHARLOTTE. Tolerate?

> (CHARLOTTE *shoves* HOWARD *playfully.* LUCINDA *shoves him in the other direction. They eat in silence for a few moments. A sense of a family portrait. A sense of a loving family.*)

Scene Two

(The dorm room, 3 a.m. Shadows and candlelight.
CHARLOTTE *and* **JONNY**. *A mostly-drunk bottle*
of whiskey.)

CHARLOTTE. I don't think they were gracious guests.

JONNY. Your mom was.

CHARLOTTE. Because she a nice Southern girl. But my dad
was born, and will always be, a rude New Yorker.

JONNY. A pushy Jew.

CHARLOTTE. Hey.

JONNY. What? You've said it a thousand times. Nothing
wrong with being a pushy Jew. Without pushy Jews we
wouldn't have Hollywood.

CHARLOTTE. Are you going to say we run the banks too?

JONNY. Your impersonation of my mother would sound
totally racist to anyone else. But there is trust here.

CHARLOTTE. *(her impersonation)* "Sweet Jesus, I'm full as a
tick and that's 'cause I'm blessed."

JONNY. She doesn't *like* to talk on the phone. Your dad
doesn't understand. She's not a phone person. She has
to come all the way down the stairs to answer. That's
how much she isn't a phone person, she doesn't have a
phone in her bedroom.

CHARLOTTE. How's she doing?

JONNY. Chemo isn't very *nice.* But it's shrinking the thing
down, so…

CHARLOTTE. The doctors confirmed that?

JONNY. What do you mean?

CHARLOTTE. I know your mom likes to look on the bright
side, that's all.

JONNY. She said the doctor said it's shrinking.

CHARLOTTE. That's good.

JONNY. It was really controlling the way your dad did that.

CHARLOTTE. Did what?

JONNY. Made me call her. He's such a *dad*.

CHARLOTTE. I know.

JONNY. If he's not careful I'm going to write a really vicious paper about him.

CHARLOTTE. Don't.

JONNY. Why?

CHARLOTTE. Because he's mine.

JONNY. There's a lot of racism in his books, you know that?

CHARLOTTE. No, I do not know that.

JONNY. Shiny black body. That's a phrase he uses. A lot.

CHARLOTTE. Is that racist?

JONNY. Fetishistic.

CHARLOTTE. It's not fair that it's the same word for fetishism as it is for like…lynching people. There should be as many words for racism as the Eskimos have for snow.

JONNY. It's all racism.

CHARLOTTE. It's all snow.

JONNY. What he doesn't get is my mom doesn't *want* me seeing her when she's sick like this. She told me very clearly, she's glad I'm not around. She *told* me to apply for the Finnish Exchange. I know your dad thinks I should drop out of school and take care of her –

CHARLOTTE. He doesn't. He thinks you should call her more often but that's a cultural thing. That's to do with Jews. And telephones.

JONNY. She's getting good care. The prognosis is good. The doctor said chemo's just a precaution.

CHARLOTTE. How can it be a precaution if it's shrinking the thing?

JONNY. Tell your dad I write to her, letters sometimes. Whenever I see something I think she might appreciate, I write it down and I mail a letter to her. How many sons do that?

CHARLOTTE. What kind of things do you think she'll appreciate?

JONNY. Like…last spring I saw someone planting crocuses on campus. And they looked real pretty. And they're her favorite flower, so… I told her about it. And she wrote back, asking about what type of crocuses and what kind of light they were getting and how long they'd last. So I found out the answers from a gardener. And I wrote her what he told me. And it was like this whole exchange we had on paper. And it was really beautiful because it was about her favorite flower. Tell your dad that happened.

CHARLOTTE. You tell him. *(beat)* Do you think maybe you should cry?

JONNY. What?

CHARLOTTE. You looked like you were going to cry.

JONNY. I'm not.

CHARLOTTE. You should drink more. Because it can be a release. It's healthy in that way. Like, Bacchanalia. That was necessary, according to Romans, because it was like an organized forum to be insane. Due to drunkenness. Every so often people need to get wasted so they can just let it all go and just fucking feel what they're feeling. And maybe that's joy and maybe that's a profound sadness, but for the Romans, and I agree, it was very necessary to let it out.

JONNY. If I drink more I'll get the hiccups.

CHARLOTTE. You have to push past the hiccups. To the release.

JONNY. Hiccups are embarrassing and make me want to go home.

CHARLOTTE. But when you're with me, when you're just with me, it's okay. Look, I know I'm a very intense individual. I cry often. I tried to kill myself when I was nine. But I think you're sad too. There's something inside everyone that needs to get out. If you don't let it out, it kills you.

JONNY. What do you think's inside me?

CHARLOTTE. I think you're real sad about your mom. I think you're real sad you never knew your dad, even though you never talk about it.

JONNY. Indeed, I am. I am sad about those things.

> *(Somehow, she awkwardly strokes his hair. He awkwardly lets himself put his head in her lap. All of this is a pause...until:)*

But that doesn't mean I have anything to say. Sometimes words are so...like most people most of the time are opening and closing their mouths and saying *nothing*.

> *(beat)*

CHARLOTTE. You don't mean me, right?

JONNY. No. But like, pretty much everyone else at this school.

CHARLOTTE. Agreed.

JONNY. Sometimes I think that the only way to be truthful is to say nothing at all.

> *(Silence until they feel certain they are living in a truthful moment together.)*

CHARLOTTE. Jonny? We're so lucky to have us. I feel like we're this model of how the world should be, you know? I'm a Jewish girl and you're a Christian boy. You're black and I'm white. But when we're together, we're so beyond that. It's so pure. I feel like people should study us.

JONNY. There should totally be a documentary about us. *(beat)* I got invited to this midnight screening of *Psycho* at the Af. Am. House. People were gonna dress up, bring snacks. I should've totally gone. But all I want to do is hang out with you. That's all I really want to ever do.

CHARLOTTE. Same.

> *(Pause. **CHARLOTTE** shakes her head from side to side. Something's upsetting her.)*

Something is happening to me and it's not going away.

(**JONNY** *sits up again, anxious.*)

JONNY. What is it?

CHARLOTTE. There's a girl. And I like her.

JONNY. Okay.

CHARLOTTE. No, I mean I like her. I *like* her.

JONNY. And I mean… "okay."

CHARLOTTE. I like her.

JONNY. Does she know?

CHARLOTTE. No. I mean, *I* didn't know. I mean, I knew I liked her but I didn't know I liked her in my *vagina*. And I've been reading a lot of feminist theory for this class I'm taking and I thought maybe it's the literature, because, you know, I agree.

JONNY. You told me in high school you were bi-sexual.

CHARLOTTE. I meant in theory. I said in theory we all are.

JONNY. I never thought it was theoretical.

(**CHARLOTTE** *holds* **JONNY**'s *hand, plays with his fingers.*)

CHARLOTTE. This girl would sleep with me if she knew I liked her. She's *actually* gay.

JONNY. How do you know?

CHARLOTTE. She has a shaved head.

JONNY. *Her?*

CHARLOTTE. You know her?

JONNY. She's the only girl in the school with a shaved head.

CHARLOTTE. Claire.

JONNY. Right. Claire. *Claire?*

CHARLOTTE. I know. I don't understand it either. She's not cute.

JONNY. Well. She's…butch.

CHARLOTTE. I do not understand how I can be attracted to her. It's gross.

JONNY. Do you think she's attracted to you?

CHARLOTTE. She smiled at me. *(beat)* She's so fucking brave with her shaved head. *(beat)* She asked me a question and she touched my arm. And when she did…

JONNY. What?

CHARLOTTE. I felt this…white light.

JONNY. You need to drink a lot more all the time because evidently you are repressing something that needs to happen.

CHARLOTTE. I love you so much. Thank you for listening to all of this.

JONNY. You don't need to be so freaked out.

CHARLOTTE. I don't even know *how* to have sex with a woman.

JONNY. *(a joke)* There's a tremendous amount of information available on the internet.

CHARLOTTE. You know, I have her cell phone number.

JONNY. You have her *number?*

CHARLOTTE. She gave it to me. In case I wanted to study with her.

JONNY. She hit on you!

CHARLOTTE. She's totally recruiting me. *(beat)* Should I call her?

JONNY. This white light, Charlotte. You should explore this white light. We don't live in medieval times, Charlotte. You're not going to be hanged for a witch.

CHARLOTTE. Unless I move to Uganda.

JONNY. It's not a big deal.

CHARLOTTE. Two related observations. First, it is insane you saying it's not a big deal because you definitely think sex is a *very* big deal because you're still a virgin. So second, maybe you don't think it's a big deal because it's two women we're talking about and you don't count it as real sex. Which makes you a sexist, homophobic pig.

JONNY. OK. First, I am being reassuring to you because you are obviously stressed out and I don't think it is a big deal for you to have sex with Claire because you are *not* a virgin and therefore you don't have to worry about who to do it with for the first time. You chose for your first time to be with that weird wanna-be stand-up comic guy you went to Israel Camp with. I absolutely think lesbian sex is real sex, of course I do. I'm just saying…don't freak out about it. It's OK.

> *(pause)*

CHARLOTTE. Amy asked me if *you* were gay.

JONNY. Amy, who I dated freshman year?

CHARLOTTE. Uh huh, she didn't understand why you didn't sleep with her.

JONNY. Because she was gross.

CHARLOTTE. Then why did you go out with her?

JONNY. I didn't know she was gross until I started to go out with her. I told you. She kept potato chips under her bed in case she wanted to snack in the night. Her sheets were covered in crumbs. And she had very dry skin, it was medical, it was eczema, so you never even knew what was in the bed. Crumbs or flaked-off skin.

CHARLOTTE. But according to received wisdom, you're a young bundle of hormones, Jonny. You didn't want to explode into Amy? For the relief?

JONNY. *(an edge to his voice)* Just because you want to sleep with a woman you don't get to do that gay thing when you assume everyone else is gay and not telling.

CHARLOTTE. I'm just asking. All the guys I know –

JONNY. Are assholes. It's probably why you want to sleep with Claire.

CHARLOTTE. *(anxious)* It's not because I'm gay?

JONNY. You're not gay, you're just cool. Look, I'm not like other guys. That's why you like me. And you're not like other girls. You're not like *anyone*. So yeah, it doesn't surprise me that you're bisexual. I have always been very uncool. Hence, still a virgin. I tried to have sex with Janelle but she was too Christian.

CHARLOTTE. You should date a nice Jew.

JONNY. Unfortunately, my favorite Jew is a lesbian.

CHARLOTTE. Bi-sexual. In theory, currently.

JONNY. I'm not going to graduate a virgin. That's too…
like, I don't want to have to tell my son that. There's a
girl. Monique. I have my eye on her.

CHARLOTTE. Great. You lose your heterosexual virginity to
Monique. I'll lose my gay virginity to Claire. And we'll
text each other in the middle to see how it's going.

JONNY. Deal.

> (*A beat.* **CHARLOTTE** *stands decisively. Her world
> is unsteady for a moment.*)

You okay?

> (*She turns on [or up?] some music.*)

CHARLOTTE. Let's dance!

> (*She pulls* **JONNY** *to his feet.*)

I always feel self-conscious dancing. I'm sick of it! I'm
sick of feeling self-conscious all the time. And it's just
you, right? We've known each other for years. We've
known each other for ten years!

JONNY. Twelve, and I don't want to dance.

CHARLOTTE. Look. Listen. I'm a terrible dancer. Okay?
But I'm going to do it and I'd like it if you'd join. This
will be my first time, dancing unselfconsciously with
another person in the room.

> (*And with that, she begins to dance. She's not
> good. She's not bad. There's something painfully
> beautiful about her attempt to be free.*)

Dance!

> (**JONNY** *joins in. There's some hand clapping,
> some finger snapping, no natural talent and it's
> sweet.*)

Why can some people just dance?

JONNY. Because they're shallow.

(CHARLOTTE laughs.)

CHARLOTTE. How bad do I look?

JONNY. Better than me. We have to turn this down, it's 3 a.m.

(He turns down [or off?] the music.)

Let me tell you something about racism. The world expecting me to be able to dance just because I'm black. That is racist. It's not an inherent ability. *(He stops dancing.)* It's like in your dad's books. All the black people can dance. Like...there's a passage about all these black people dancing at a club in New Orleans and it's totally stereotypical. They're like...rhythmically gyrating.

CHARLOTTE. I've seen black people rhythmically gyrate. Not in this room, but...

JONNY. You know why you're so scared of sleeping with Claire?

CHARLOTTE. Because it's sexually deviant and also she has no hair on her head, only under her arms?

JONNY. *(He stops dancing.)* Your father's fifth book, *Snow on Peachtree Street,* don't you remember what it was about?

CHARLOTTE. Well knowing my Dad's oeuvre as I do: someone was murdered and Detective Grayson investigates and it's not the first guy he talks to, it's not the second guy, it's not the third guy, it's definitely the fourth guy, definitely the fourth guy – oh no wait...it was the second guy.

JONNY. Actually the plotting is more sophisticated than that but... *(beat)* He wrote about the tree. The big tree in your yard. I remember hearing the description and thinking hey, that's our tree. But instead of a tire hanging there was a body hanging. And I thought maybe it was a lynching because my mom said they lynched a man on that tree one time. But it was a white girl hanging. Detective Grayson thought she was a murder victim. But it was a red herring. Because later it turned out she'd killed herself. Because she was a lesbian.

CHARLOTTE. I haven't even read that one, so

JONNY. All I'm saying is, your dad is a little bit racist, and a little bit homophobic.

CHARLOTTE. So is everyone's dad.

JONNY. How would I know?

CHARLOTTE. Tell me a secret, Jonny. You know all my secrets, now. I'm in love with a girl.

JONNY. In love?

CHARLOTTE. What if I'm not bi-sexual. What if I'm lesbian?

JONNY. Then…good. You can get fat and pretend it's a political statement.

(beat) Call her. Take her out. I hear there's a Joan Baez concert coming to town.

CHARLOTTE. Shall I do it right now?

JONNY. Go for it!

> (**CHARLOTTE** *has her cell phone out.*)

CHARLOTTE. I feel like I'm about to jump off a cliff.

JONNY. You might not be into it. Four breasts may be two too many.

CHARLOTTE. *(yelling)* I want you to lose your virginity!

JONNY. I will. ASAP.

CHARLOTTE. I want you to lose it to me.

JONNY. But you're a lesbian.

CHARLOTTE. You love me.

JONNY. But I don't find you sexy.

CHARLOTTE. *(angry)* You always say it's like incest but it's *not*.

> (**CHARLOTTE** *does something to her phone, then throws it across the room.*)

I erased her number. If this is a fucking phase, I'm going to let it pass without actually *doing* it. If I'm bi-sexual then I just want to be with men.

JONNY. Okay. That's valid.

CHARLOTTE. Jonny, we have to do it sometime.

JONNY. Why do we? Because you've gotten really drunk?

CHARLOTTE. Because we're a man and a woman. We love each other. It's just inevitable. Doesn't it feel inevitable to you?

JONNY. It feels like an inevitable way to ruin the friendship.

CHARLOTTE. Why does it have to ruin anything? Let's just try it. And if we don't want to keep doing it together, with each other, then when we belong to other people, it'll be something they can't take away. But we might like it, Jonny. It might be amazing. We might get married and live happily ever after.

(She undresses.)

JONNY. It wouldn't work. I want to bring my kids up Christian. And...black. You want to bring your kids up Jewish. We've talked about this.

CHARLOTTE. (talking over him) Oh look beyond. Let's get beyond fucking tribal thinking, can we? Please. Let's be the fucking future, Jonny. On a basic biological level, you must be attracted to me, right? I'm a twenty-one year old girl. I know I don't dress all sexy, but look. No clothes. This is prime meat. Everything sags starting next year. Capitalize now.

JONNY. You are very, very drunk right now. You're slurring.

(That's not true. She is not slurring.)

CHARLOTTE. (angry) You said you wanted to lose your virginity before the end of college. You're just scared. It's your defining fucking feature. You know how we go to the fair every year and you won't get on a single ride, you just watch me? Do you want that to be your whole fucking life? Climb on board!

JONNY. If I had sex with you right now it would be like date rape.

CHARLOTTE. (angry) Why won't you give us a chance? We love each other. We are everything to each other. When

I'm with you the whole world can go fuck itself. That's what it feels like to be in real love! We're in love, Jonny. We should get fucking married and have babies and talk and touch and talk and touch and stop wasting time.

(She walks or dances towards him, trying to be sexy. She comes over to him, kisses him.)

Stop. Thinking.

(She rushes away, rips off her underwear and lies on the bed.)

OK. Now get over here and fuck me right now.

(She lies on the bed and stares straight up at the ceiling, ready.)

This is something we absolutely should do, Jonny. I know you're a virgin but I've never come with a guy before so I'm like a virgin in a way. Emotionally, I'm a virgin. I can come by myself and I've always been too embarrassed to show them how to do it but I could show you and I wouldn't be embarrassed because it's just you. And we could be good. And comfortable. Don't you want to be comfortable?

JONNY. I want so much more than that.

(She looks over.)

*(Painful moments as **CHARLOTTE** registers the rejection. Covers herself. **JONNY** can't bring himself to leave her like this, sits next to her, puts an arm around her.)*

Scene Three

*(Day. **CHARLOTTE**'s family living room. Space. Money, taste, comfort, light. Off this room, exits to other implied locations in the large house. A sense of flow through the space.)*

*(**JONNY** stands alone in the middle of the room. Eventually, a grim **HOWARD** enters carrying a bucket. He barely acknowledges **JONNY** as he passes by, through and out to the kitchen. **JONNY** checks the time. He seems a little pissed.)*

*(**LUCINDA** enters.)*

LUCINDA. *(hushed)* Do you have a light, sugar?

JONNY. What?

LUCINDA. *(louder)* Do you have a light?

JONNY. I don't smoke.

LUCINDA. Must have been a fun night. Until she threw up all over the rose bushes. She's still sleeping it off.

JONNY. I'm here for Howard. And actually, I have to go soon. My mom's cooking a ham.

LUCINDA. I'm sure Howard will just be a few more minutes. He's just trying to rescue the roses. Because it's probably not good for them. Vomit.

JONNY. I don't know. They say manure...

LUCINDA. It's not the same. Because of acids.

JONNY. That makes sense.

> *(**HOWARD** enters with the bucket. The bucket is now full of water.)*

HOWARD. *(to **JONNY**)* I know you kids drink at your age. And I know it's spring break. But this is not OK.

> *(He exits.)*

LUCINDA. If you want him in a better mood, compare him to Hitchcock again. He thinks it's the insight of the century. *(beat)* How's your head?

JONNY. Fine.

LUCINDA. I guess you guys were just out having fun and had a few too many.

JONNY. *(non-committal)* Yeah.

LUCINDA. She was pretty upset when she got home. Do you know what she was upset about?

JONNY. She was fine when we left her.

LUCINDA. You left her?

JONNY. She ran into other friends and stayed out.

LUCINDA. She's fragile, you know.

(**HOWARD** *returns with the empty bucket.*)

HOWARD. *(to* **JONNY***)* I'm sorry I've kept you waiting. I just didn't expect you to be here on time. Charlotte's still sleeping it off.

LUCINDA. He wasn't with her.

HOWARD. What?

LUCINDA. *(beat)* Well, if anyone wants me I'll be in the sunroom.

(**LUCINDA** *exits.*)

HOWARD. I thought she was out with you.

JONNY. She was, but then a whole load of kids from high school showed up and Monique didn't want to stay and neither did I. Charlotte did. She was totally sober the last I saw her.

HOWARD. The thing is, Jonny, you're like a brother to her, right?

JONNY. Yeah.

HOWARD. So act like it. You don't leave a lady alone in a bar.

JONNY. *(beat)* You know, if we could get to this interview I'd appreciate it. My mom's cooking a ham and she's going to a lot of trouble.

HOWARD. Your mom's up and about, huh? That's got to feel good.

JONNY. It is Easter.

HOWARD. *(astonished)* Is it? Today?

JONNY. Yes.

HOWARD. Well, happy Easter!

JONNY. Anyway. *(deep breath, ready to get down to business)* Thank you for doing this.

HOWARD. Sure. Sure. You know, Jonny. She talked about you last night.

JONNY. She did?

HOWARD. Briefly. Want to know what she said?

JONNY. Not right now.

HOWARD. "I love him."

JONNY. Huh.

HOWARD. She mumbled it. She shouted it. Then she passed out.

JONNY. She said "him," right? She might not have meant me?

HOWARD. My daughter is in love with you.

JONNY. No, she isn't.

HOWARD. I can see what's in front of my face. It's no coincidence I write detective fiction. Ever since you started dating your new lady friend –

JONNY. Monique –

HOWARD. Charlotte has been off her food. Pale. Depressed. Won't talk to me, won't talk to Lula. But it's pretty obvious what the problem is.

JONNY. Charlotte and I are just friends.

HOWARD. *(beat)* You'd be lucky to have her.

JONNY. *(beat)* I'm not comfortable talking about her like this.

HOWARD. I met Monique. Let's talk man to man.

JONNY. I don't think we should.

HOWARD. Is she really the one? Or is it just that she has enormous breasts? And listen, I get that, good for you. That's fun. But are you responding to her *beyond* that?

Because deep love, you know, that's about so much more. It's a spiritual connection. When that's not there there's nothing, you know?

JONNY. Monique and I have a spiritual connection, that's the whole –

HOWARD. Look, I know this is inappropriate. I just want to make sure that... I see between you and my daughter, I've seen... I've seen love. Real love. And I wanted to deny it. You're both so young. And she's my...she's my angel. But it's you. She's set her sights on you. And so I ask you, man to man, to consider if what you have with Monique is worth giving up the joy you could have with Charlotte for, who knows, the rest of your life.

(Pause. JONNY tries to figure out how to address all this.)

JONNY. It's not just about her breasts.

HOWARD. I see. Tell me.

JONNY. This is about family. I know you respect that. I am a Baptist.

HOWARD. *(seeing the light)* Aaaah...

JONNY. You don't want Charlotte marrying a Baptist and having little Christian babies, I know you don't want that.

HOWARD. Charlotte cannot be a Baptist. That is out of the question.

JONNY. She and I are not an option.

HOWARD. But at heart, we are all just people.

JONNY. I've got to get this interview done. It's half my grade.

HOWARD. Lucinda is not a Jew. Yes, she converted and I appreciate that, but she is not a Jew. At best, she is an extraordinarily lapsed Catholic. And although we define ourselves as Jews, our life is not very Jewish. You know that. I would *prefer* that Charlotte be with someone that defines themselves as a Jew. But above all, she must be happy. And if happiness to her is being with you,

and if you're just worrying about your mother, then I
implore you. Find a way. How long have I known you?

JONNY. Since I was nine.

HOWARD. This is the first time since you were nine years old
that you have earned my respect. Your religion, your
faith, your mother, those are concerns of substance.
I admire them. Hey, more than that, I *get* it. I'm the
same! My father's father was a rabbi! A *Polish* rabbi.
Beard. Side curls. The whole nine yards. If he could
have heard me talking this way it would have broken
his heart. But fucking tribalism? I'm not for it. My wife.
Lucinda. I turned, I saw her, I fucking *inhaled* her spirit
and I was a dead man. God is love. You know that. And
when I saw you with Monique it was clear, Jonny: there's
no love there. There's no spark. There's just two black
kids trying to do the right things by their parents. Life's
too short for that shit. Know what I mean? What is that
smell? Do you smell something?

JONNY. Yeah. Marijuana.

HOWARD. *(baffled)* Where's it coming from?

JONNY. *(awkwardly)* The sunroom?

> *(beat)*

HOWARD. Excuse me.

> **(HOWARD** *exits.* **CHARLOTTE** *is at the doorway
> that leads to upstairs.)*

CHARLOTTE. Am I dreaming or is someone getting high?

> *(They look at each other for a few moments before:)*

JONNY. Your mom, I think.

CHARLOTTE. What are you doing here?

JONNY. My paper.

CHARLOTTE. I'm in a lot of pain.

JONNY. You know, your dad's going to be back in a second
and there's already been a lot of distractions and I'd be
grateful if you didn't suck out all of the energy in the
room. If I don't have a paper I flunk.

CHARLOTTE. I feel so nauseous.

JONNY. You really hurt my feelings last night. And you embarrassed me.

CHARLOTTE. I'm sorry, I don't remember.

JONNY. You don't remember anything?

CHARLOTTE. I remember a lot of shouting. I remember I was crying and you left me. Downtown. Did you leave me downtown? On the street?

JONNY. Yes.

> (**JONNY** *is trying to decide whether or not to give in when* **LUCINDA** *and* **HOWARD** *enter.*)

LUCINDA. I have to smoke something, Howard. I need a fucking crutch, alright. I need one.

HOWARD. I bought you an electronic cigarette!

LUCINDA. You're like a spy, you know that? Following me around, checking up on me.

HOWARD. It was supposed to be a secret? That stuff stinks. Where'd you get it?

LUCINDA. *(exaggerated Southern accent)* I went down to the docks, Detective Grayson. I sold myself to a young man in blue. While he was sleeping, I stole his marijuana. Don't arrest me, please God don't arrest me, I'll do anything! Anything!

> *(beat)*

HOWARD. What is that?

LUCINDA. That was supposed to be: stop *badgering* me.

HOWARD. Is that supposed to be funny?

LUCINDA. Uh huh, exactly. It was a joke.

HOWARD. A joke, like a parody of my work?

LUCINDA. You put the work out there, the public will judge it.

HOWARD. You're not the *public*. You're my wife.

JONNY. I'm here.

HOWARD. Yes we know you're here.

JONNY. Oh.

CHARLOTTE. Did I wake you guys last night?

LUCINDA. How are you feeling, honey?

CHARLOTTE. How do I look?

LUCINDA. I'll get you some aspirin.

>   (LUCINDA *exits.*)

HOWARD. You absolutely woke us last night.

CHARLOTTE. Let's talk about it later. I'll go to the kitchen. I don't want to suck all of the air out of the room. I know you men have important business.

HOWARD. You scared me.

CHARLOTTE. I'm sorry.

HOWARD. That was too drunk. If you have a problem –

CHARLOTTE. I don't.

HOWARD. A drinking problem or a problem that's making you drink, you come to me. We talk about it.

CHARLOTTE. OK.

HOWARD. I'm your dad. There's no problem I won't help you fix.

JONNY. Howard, we really need to –

HOWARD. One second, please Jonny. *(to* CHARLOTTE*)* If you came home and said, "I murdered someone," I would say, "Where's the corpse?" Then I'd cut it in tiny pieces and feed it to barnyard animals. And if by some miracle the police found you anyway, I'd say I did it.

CHARLOTTE. I think the better parenting choice would be to make me take responsibility for the crime.

HOWARD. I'd never let you get the chair.

CHARLOTTE. I'm in love with a woman.

>   (*pause*)

HOWARD. Jonny, I'm going to have to ask you to come back.

JONNY. Right.

HOWARD. We'll find another time.

JONNY. Sure. Great.

> (**LUCINDA** *enters and hands a glass and aspirin*
> **CHARLOTTE**. **JONNY** *starts to exit.*)

CHARLOTTE. *(weakly)* Can you stay, Jonny?

> (**JONNY** *has no intention of staying. He gets his
> things together.*)

LUCINDA. *(brightly)* Did you get what you need, honey?

> (**JONNY** *ignores her, exits.* **CHARLOTTE** *washes
> down the aspirin. Chokes.*)

CHARLOTTE. Is this vodka?

LUCINDA. Hair of the dog, sugar-pie.

HOWARD. Are you fucking serious?

> (**HOWARD** *snatches the glass away from*
> **CHARLOTTE.**)

LUCINDA. It works. I'm trying to help.

HOWARD. Then be a mother. Your daughter has something
to tell you.

CHARLOTTE. No, I don't.

HOWARD. Yes, you do.

CHARLOTTE. I don't. I shouldn't have said anything. It
doesn't matter. This isn't something we need to have a
family summit about.

HOWARD. I think it is.

CHARLOTTE. Why?

HOWARD. Because… I don't know. Because it sounds like
something we should have a conversation about. *(to*
LUCINDA*)* She's not in love with Jonny. She's in love
with…

CHARLOTTE. Claire.

LUCINDA. *(intrigued)* Who's he?

HOWARD. A woman.

LUCINDA. *(fascinated)* Really?

> (**LUCINDA** *produces a half-smoked joint from her
> pocket, lights up.*)

HOWARD. Really?

LUCINDA. Really.

CHARLOTTE. Since when do you smoke pot?

LUCINDA. Since I quit nicotine for your father.

HOWARD. It stinks.

LUCINDA. You used to love smoking pot.

HOWARD. We're talking about Charlotte.

LUCINDA. Honey, she's in college. Everyone experiments, in college. That's what you were, at first. My Jewish experiment. *(to* **CHARLOTTE***)* I've slept with a woman.

HOWARD. Oh Jesus.

CHARLOTTE. *(shocked, to* **HOWARD***)* Did you know that?

LUCINDA. Honey, he was there.

CHARLOTTE. This isn't like that. This isn't that.

HOWARD. *(to* **CHARLOTTE***)* I just like clarity, OK? Just so I understand what we're talking about here. Are you gay?

CHARLOTTE. I don't know. Probably not. Maybe. I don't know. I'm in love with someone named Claire. And it's been going on for a while. And it turns out that when you're in love you want to tell everybody. But I felt like I shouldn't, I kept thinking we'd break up and nobody needs to know it ever happened, but we keep not breaking up, we're really in love and so now I have to tell you guys. Because I love you. I'm so sorry. I know this is not what you want for me.

HOWARD. *(quickly)* We don't care. *(to* **LUCINDA***)* Do you care? *(to* **CHARLOTTE***)* I don't care.

LUCINDA. If you were gay, that's fine. But you are not a lesbian. I promise you.

CHARLOTTE. How do you know?

LUCINDA. You're just *not*. Remember all through high school you had a crush on Mr. Conner. You were obsessed with him. And there was that boy, that boy you liked. Edward. Little gay girls have crushes on girls, honey.

CHARLOTTE. Yeah.

LUCINDA. You're just a free spirit and your father and I love that about you.

HOWARD. You know about twenty years ago I was in the West Village in Manhattan eating a popsicle and this guy with very short shorts, beautiful young man, bare-chested, smiled at me from across the street and he called out, "Can I have a suck on your popsicle?" And I knew what he meant.

LUCINDA. No kidding.

HOWARD. I have always wished that I had the courage to experiment. Like a real artist. *(to* **CHARLOTTE***)* I'm very proud of you.

CHARLOTTE. I want you to meet Claire. Can I bring her home for a weekend?

*(***LUCINDA** *and* **HOWARD** *exchange quick glances.)*

LUCINDA. Well of course, honey.

HOWARD. Great. Can't wait to meet Claire.

LUCINDA. Do you have a picture?

CHARLOTTE. Do you really want to see a picture?

LUCINDA. Yes!

*(***CHARLOTTE** *goes over to a laptop and logs into her Facebook page.)*

CHARLOTTE. She's not, I guess, super cute in the conventional sense. But she's very smart. And Dad, she's half-Jewish.

HOWARD. Well, hooray.

*(***CHARLOTTE** *shows them the picture.)*

CHARLOTTE. Here.

*(***HOWARD** *and* **LUCINDA** *take in the photograph.)*

LUCINDA. Now *she* is a lesbian.

CHARLOTTE. You see? That's not nice. You say it like an insult.

LUCINDA. No, I just mean she is definitely…her mother would not be able to reassure her that –

CHARLOTTE. Who says I want reassurance?

> *(beat)*

HOWARD. Honey, however you want to be. Whoever you want to be with. We love you.

LUCINDA. Although if you're going to be with a woman, why would you want to be with a woman who looks like a man? I don't get it.

CHARLOTTE. I don't get it either. But I can't stop.

> *(beat)*

LUCINDA. Do you want to stop?

CHARLOTTE. Yes.

LUCINDA. Why?

CHARLOTTE. BECAUSE SHE'S NOT WHO I AM!

> **(CHARLOTTE** *runs up the stairs. Pause.* **LUCINDA** *takes a hit off the joint.)*

HOWARD. Huh.

LUCINDA. While things are in pieces, I'm seeing someone.

> **(HOWARD** *freezes. Pause.)*

HOWARD. Whatever we say next we will say quietly and carefully. I will not have her more upset.

LUCINDA. She's not a kid any more, Howard.

HOWARD. She's my kid. *(beat)* You remember those wrists? Those skinny white bug-bitten nine-year-old arms and those wrists. And the promises we made.

LUCINDA. I'm sorry. But she's all grown up.

> **(HOWARD** *takes difficult breaths.)*

HOWARD. Jesus, what is happening?

Scene Four

(Still the living room. Late. Dark. **CHARLOTTE** *and* **JONNY**. **JONNY** *is cold.)*

CHARLOTTE. How was Easter?

JONNY. I can't just hang out.

CHARLOTTE. I know.

JONNY. I've got company.

CHARLOTTE. I get it. *(beat)* I said bring Monique.

JONNY. Monique doesn't want to see you.

CHARLOTTE. Wow.

JONNY. You were a total asshole. To her. To me.

CHARLOTTE. You have to get over it.

JONNY. It was less than twenty-four hours ago, so I don't think I have to get over it right now.

CHARLOTTE. I need you to get over it by the time we get back to school. I was drunk.

JONNY. So? *In vino veritas.* Ever hear that saying?

CHARLOTTE. Everyone's heard that saying.

JONNY. How much do you remember of what you said?

CHARLOTTE. You know what I remember? I was upset and I needed you to be there for me.

JONNY. You have a problem with selfishness.

CHARLOTTE. Jonny? Don't break up with me.

JONNY. We're not together.

CHARLOTTE. Yes we are.

JONNY. Here's what I'm starting to think. You have real psychological problems.

CHARLOTTE. Obviously I do. I tried to kill myself when I was nine.

JONNY. But I mean now. You have real problems now.

CHARLOTTE. So?

JONNY. So they're becoming unmanageable. For me.

CHARLOTTE. Oh my God.

JONNY. Look it's not my job to…

CHARLOTTE. To what?

JONNY. You make being your friend a job.

CHARLOTTE. Oh.

JONNY. I'm just being honest.

CHARLOTTE. Well good because honesty is key.

JONNY. All I do is pick you up. And before, I had no one else. Now I do. I have someone. And how do you think it makes her feel, if I'm running around after you all the time?

CHARLOTTE. Jealous?

JONNY. No, not jealous. It disgusts her. It makes her feel like a girl that's not my girlfriend is running my life.

CHARLOTTE. That's what she says?

JONNY. Yes.

CHARLOTTE. And you *let* her say that? You didn't stand up for us? You know that *I* am seeing someone –

I would never let Claire come between us. I don't think who you fuck is more important than your best friend.

JONNY. Well I'm not *fucking* Monique so there's that. Because we're looking for something a little deeper. *We* are looking to be best friends. Because that's what a relationship is. So I know you and Claire never stop fucking, and I know it's the most incredible thing that's ever happened to you and I am happy for you, I really am. But it is time to accept that our road has divided. Different journeys. Different destinations. For sure.

CHARLOTTE. I'm off on the road less travelled all by myself, huh?

JONNY. You don't even like me. Did you know that? You told me last night.

CHARLOTTE. Because *I'm* jealous. I'm jealous of Monique. You have to let people behave badly sometimes.

JONNY. You have a drinking problem. And by the way so does Claire.

CHARLOTTE. Thank you for telling me that. That's what friends do.

JONNY. Monique can't believe I'm over here tonight. Neither can my mom.

CHARLOTTE. Your mom knows we had a fight?

JONNY. We didn't have a fight, Charlotte. You screamed at me in the street like a drunken maniac for fifteen minutes. And I tried to calm you down and put you in a cab and you tried to make out with me. In front of my girlfriend. And when I pushed you off, which was the only way to get you off, you tried to call the cops. And then you told Monique I was gay. Because I wouldn't fuck you that time. Because I don't fuck her. And you said it was extra proof that I was gay that I wouldn't fuck her because she has such enormous breasts. And she explained to you, as I have done like a thousand times, that we don't fuck because we're Christians. And you told her the two of you, just her and you, should go off and find another bar and really talk about that because you found it impossible to believe that any intelligent person truly believed in the risen Christ.

(*pause*)

CHARLOTTE. Huh.

JONNY. And I think you meant all that.

CHARLOTTE. Jonny, she really does have enormous breasts.

JONNY. That's one of the things I like about her. When we are married, I will engage with them more fully.

CHARLOTTE. You are *not* getting married.

JONNY. I think that we will.

CHARLOTTE. That's ridiculous.

JONNY. See! You meant every word you said so how can we be friends?

CHARLOTTE. I don't think you're gay. I'm sorry.

JONNY. You're sorry you're gay and you're taking it out on everyone else.

CHARLOTTE. Do you really think I'm gay?

JONNY. I can't talk about this any more. I can't. Ever! I can't give it a single second of my time. I'm really happy you told your parents. I told you they'd be cool. I have to go.

CHARLOTTE. Can I see your mom before school starts up?

JONNY. Why?

CHARLOTTE. To say good-bye.

JONNY. Not while Monique's there.

CHARLOTTE. But school starts Tuesday. *(beat)* You shouldn't have told her about last night. Gossip's a sin.

JONNY. You know what my mom said? She said, "That child's always been troubled." She's praying for *you*, Charlotte. While churches across the nation are praying for her.

CHARLOTTE. Prayer doesn't do any good, Jonny. Magic doesn't exist. Grow up!

>   *(silence)*

> We're over, aren't we?

JONNY. Fucking done.

>   *(He exits.)*

CHARLOTTE. Jonny!

>   *(Loud, loud music. A woman's voice. Religious. Etta James "At Last,"* maybe. But soaring.)*

>   (**CHARLOTTE** *runs after* **JONNY.** *We fluidly transition into:*)

Scene Five

(Outside. Moonlight. A huge tree. An ancient thick rope hanging from a branch, a tire at the end.)

(JONNY is waiting under the tree. He's in a dark suit. He's in despair.)

(CHARLOTTE comes out. She's barefoot, in a loose, cotton nightgown. Cautious. They stare at each other for a few moments.)

(JONNY makes a gesture that says, "Here I am." A sort of helpless shrug.)

CHARLOTTE. I'm so sorry for your loss.

(pause)

Have you cried?

(JONNY shakes his head.)

You should cry a lot. As she's dead. You didn't cry at the funeral.

JONNY. And you weren't invited.

CHARLOTTE. That's why I sat at the back.

(beat)

JONNY. I was happy you were there.

(beat)

CHARLOTTE. I kept looking at you. You never looked back.

(beat)

JONNY. So you know I'm engaged?

CHARLOTTE. Yes. Congratulations. I hope you'll be very happy. Really.

JONNY. I can't get married.

CHARLOTTE. Why not?

JONNY. Because I did something bad.

(beat)

CHARLOTTE. What did you do?

JONNY. I had sex with a guy that I hate who's really into comic books.

CHARLOTTE. What?

JONNY. I had sex with a guy that I hate who's really into comic books.

CHARLOTTE. Huh.

> *(beat)*

JONNY. Actually that is an ongoing situation.

CHARLOTTE. *(beat, then slowly)* You're having sex with a guy you hate who's really into comic books. *(beat)* As of when?

JONNY. His name is Jonah.

CHARLOTTE. Jonah.

JONNY. He's awful. *(beat)* I don't know what to do. I can't stop. He lives in a shit hole, there are roaches and a ton of musty, vintage Aquamans. I can't get married. I have no idea what I'm doing. Monique is wondering where I am right now. You have to help me. I don't want to be doing what I'm doing. I don't want to be… *(can't find the end of the sentence)* I kind of don't want to be.

CHARLOTTE. *(hesitant)* It's okay. You're okay. *(beat)* So… I'm a little confused.

JONNY. Yeah me too.

CHARLOTTE. Is Jonah your first… Gentleman Caller?

> *(pause)*

Jonny?

JONNY. I can't believe my mom's dead. I can't call her on the phone. I can't write her a letter. She's just gone. And all through the funeral I should have been thinking of her. But I wasn't. I was thinking of Edward. *(beat)* From camp?

CHARLOTTE. Edward from camp who was pretty like a girl?

> *(beat)*

JONNY. Edward who was pretty like a girl.

CHARLOTTE. He was first?

> (JONNY *nods.*)

When we were eleven? *(beat)* You knew when we were eleven?

JONNY. No! I didn't know anything! We shouldn't talk about this.

CHARLOTTE. I think you want to talk. I think that's why you're loitering in my yard.

> *(pause)*

JONNY. My mom's in a box, I wish it was me. I'm going to hell, you know that?

CHARLOTTE. There's no such thing as hell, you know that?

> *(beat)*

JONNY. It was Edward's idea. And I don't know why. I don't know why he looked at me and was like – yeah. You. What did he see?

CHARLOTTE. He saw you, Jonny. You're lovely. *(pause)* Why didn't you tell me?

JONNY. It happened one time. Just one time. And I never thought about it. I think I repressed the memory. That's why I didn't tell you. It was like… It was like ear wax, you know? Ear wax that's in so deep you forget it's there, even though it's making everything fuzzy. *(angry)* It fucked me up.

> *(pause as CHARLOTTE processes)*

CHARLOTTE. So Edward happened. Then repression?

JONNY. Yes.

CHARLOTTE. Then Jonah.

JONNY. Yeah, pretty much.

CHARLOTTE. Pretty much? *(beat, heart racing, regarding whiskey)* Did you drink all of this?

JONNY. Yeah, I'm wasted.

> *(Pause. JONNY hiccups.)*

CHARLOTTE. Pretty much? *(scared of the answer)* Have you been with guys this whole time, Jonny?

JONNY. I have *not* been with men this whole time. I've been with Monique. And before that Janelle. And before that Amy.

CHARLOTTE. A string of good Christian women. One with Eczema.

> *(pause)*

JONNY. I didn't tell you because I didn't want it to be true. When you say things out loud they become true. I say almost nothing to Jonah. And he only talks about comics. *(beat)* I've been very fucking lonely, Charlotte.

> *(Beat.* **CHARLOTTE** *controls her temper. Takes charge.)*

CHARLOTTE. Well you've said it out loud and it sounds true so you have to tell Monique.

JONNY. Tell her what?

CHARLOTTE. That you're *gay.* Jesus, poor Monique.

JONNY. *(furious)* Since when do you give a *shit* about Monique?

> *(Pause.* **JONNY** *hiccups.)*

And I'm not necessarily *gay.* Because it's not *real* if it's because someone else fucking fucked me up. I just need to get better.

CHARLOTTE. Oh Jonny.

> *(Somehow they're together now and she might be holding him.)*

JONNY. I really didn't know.

CHARLOTTE. So you've experienced the white light.

JONNY. Oh yes. Many times now. *(beat)* I heard you and Claire broke up, by the way. I'm sorry.

CHARLOTTE. Yes, it was terrible. I called you a couple of times, you never picked up. *(beat, hard)* I missed you. This has been very hard.

JONNY. For me too.

>   *(beat)*

CHARLOTTE. Claire's with men, now. She grew her hair back.

>   *(Beat. JONNY registers this. Fascinating.)*

JONNY. No way.

CHARLOTTE. Yup. She was a total LUG. Lesbian Until Graduation.

>   *(He hiccups again.)*

JONNY. Fuck these hurt. They really hurt.

CHARLOTTE. I'm going to give you a shock okay. That will get rid of them.

JONNY. OK.

>   *(They stare at each other. She punches him in the stomach. So hard. He doubles up. She stands over him. He hiccups.)*

ACT TWO

Scene One

(Five years later. Spring.)

(CHARLOTTE and JONNY at a wooden picnic table under the tree in the backyard. The table is set for lunch. Plates. Wine. The swing has gone.)

JONNY. I am *really* into the idea.

CHARLOTTE. *(thrilled)* You are?

JONNY. I'd love it.

CHARLOTTE. We don't know if we're looking for a donor or a father or something in between but we definitely want kids.

JONNY. You've always wanted kids.

CHARLOTTE. And so has she. I mean this is way down the line, she has to finish her residency so it's way too early to bring it up with you but I just wanted to tell you because Martha and I talk about it all the time, which means we talk about you, and would you, or wouldn't you.

JONNY. It makes sense. We always talked about what great parents we'd make.

CHARLOTTE. And Martha, obviously. I mean she and I would be the parents. And you'd be – I don't know. We would have to discuss it.

JONNY. We'll figure out our own rules.

CHARLOTTE. Yes we will. I should mention that Martha also has a very close friend who's a gay man and she's interested in talking to him too but I think he wants kids with his partner.

JONNY. *(disconcerted)* I guess this is all a long way off. We'll figure it out.

> (**LUCINDA** *enters from the house carrying a huge bowl of salad.*)

LUCINDA. Hey y'all!

CHARLOTTE. *(to* **JONNY***)* But I am very psyched that you're into the idea and I will tell Martha.

LUCINDA. *(sitting down)* Jesus, Jonny, you look great. You've...filled out. I don't know. Something.

JONNY. I swim a lot.

LUCINDA. In the ocean?

JONNY. The ocean. The gym.

CHARLOTTE. He looks great, doesn't he?

> (**HOWARD** *enters from the house with four glasses.*)

HOWARD. How's everybody?

CHARLOTTE. Can I do anything?

HOWARD. No, I think we're all squared away. Let's eat.

> (**HOWARD** *sits.* **JONNY** *serves himself some salad.*)

CHARLOTTE. I really think we can do the wedding back here.

HOWARD. The front yard's much bigger.

CHARLOTTE. I would rather invite fewer people, and do it back here. It's so romantic under the tree.

JONNY. Where's the tire swing?

CHARLOTTE. I took it down to see how it would look with just a chuppah back here.

HOWARD. The invitations have already been sent.

JONNY. It's better out front. The lawn is flatter. You can set up a dance floor more easily. Are we doing dancing?

CHARLOTTE. Oh yes. Dinner. Dancing. Unfortunately for me, Martha loves dancing.

LUCINDA. She's very good.

JONNY. Charlotte, you're going to have to tell me my best man duties. I mean, traditionally it would be for me to get you drunk and take you to a strip club. But you've stopped drinking.

CHARLOTTE. That doesn't mean I can't go to a strip club.

HOWARD. No one's going to a strip club. *(beat)* In my opinion. I mean, of course it's none of my business.

CHARLOTTE. Don't you want to come, Dad? Don't the dads come?

LUCINDA. I'm coming.

HOWARD. I think strip clubs degrade women. So I don't want to go. And I'm surprised you'd participate in something like that, Charlotte.

JONNY. I was actually joking. I can't think of anything worse than going to a strip club. Unless it was full of men. *(A slightly weird moment.)* We can do whatever you want.

LUCINDA. Will you be bringing a date to the wedding, Jonny?

CHARLOTTE. No, he won't.

JONNY. Excuse me?

CHARLOTTE. Jonny specializes in the three-second relationship. I don't want some dude he just met competing for attention at my wedding.

LUCINDA. Making up for lost time, huh, Jonny? Good for you.

JONNY. *(touched)* Thanks. *(beat)* I love the strawberries in the salad.

CHARLOTTE. Is there something apart from wine to pour into these glasses?

LUCINDA. Howard, where's the lemonade? I made lemonade.

HOWARD. Oh.

LUCINDA. Well, go get it.

HOWARD. Shit.

CHARLOTTE. I'll go.

LUCINDA. No you just got off a plane. Howard, go get it.

HOWARD. Anything for anybody else?

JONNY. Just the lemonade would be great.

>*(A split second of tension between* **HOWARD** *and* **JONNY**. *No one else notices.* **HOWARD** *trudges back to the house.)*

Actually I met a guy I like a couple of weeks ago. His name is Will. He's an airline pilot. Seriously, he's an airline pilot.

LUCINDA. Where'd you meet him?

JONNY. Church.

>*(The slightest of pauses.)*

CHARLOTTE. Well if you're still seeing him in three months. Maybe. As long as he doesn't distract you from your best man duties.

JONNY. You got the ceremony all figured out?

CHARLOTTE. We found a very accommodating lady rabbi. Dad did.

JONNY. That's great.

CHARLOTTE. But I need you to help me find a dress. Or pants? Do you think I should wear pants? Like a tux?

LUCINDA. Honey, you're not wearing a tux.

JONNY. A tux might be amazing.

LUCINDA. She's gay, she's not a man.

JONNY. *(to* **LUCINDA***)* What happened to your wedding dress?

LUCINDA. eBay.

CHARLOTTE. I'm bringing options home tomorrow afternoon. Everyone has to give their opinion.

JONNY. What's the guest list up to?

CHARLOTTE. Eighty.

>*(***HOWARD*** *returns with a pitcher of lemonade.)*

HOWARD. Did you tell Jonny the big news?

CHARLOTTE. I didn't know there was big news.

HOWARD. My dad's flying in from New York!

JONNY. That's great.

HOWARD. He's delighted about the whole thing!

LUCINDA. Bullshit.

HOWARD. Seriously. I was terrified to tell him. I really thought it might be the end of our relationship altogether. But he was so good about it. He actually said "mazel tov" which is more than he said when I told him I was marrying Lucinda. And he explained, and this is very interesting, that the Torah says *nothing* about two women. So Halachically speaking, it's fine!

CHARLOTTE. *(to* JONNY*)* Isn't that nice? I'm invisible.

JONNY. That beats visible and stoned to death.

HOWARD. Who's stoning you to death?

JONNY. You don't think gay men are oppressed?

HOWARD. Not by the Jews. We *get* being oppressed. So we try not to do it to other people.

JONNY. Tell it to Palestine.

HOWARD. Watch it!

LUCINDA. My Daddy had a rule. No politics at the table.

HOWARD. Otherwise known as the "if you don't agree with me, you may not speak" rule.

LUCINDA. Otherwise known as being polite.

CHARLOTTE. Can you two not bicker?

> *(beat)*

LUCINDA. I also reached out to my remaining family. They told me to go fuck myself.

CHARLOTTE. I didn't know that. *(beat)* That's nice that you reached out though.

LUCINDA. Fuck them.

HOWARD. *(to* JONNY*)* You know Martha's Jewish?

JONNY. I did know that.

LUCINDA. She is whip smart. And very pretty. Can't wait to have her in the family. A surgeon! I really get off on telling people that. I say, "My daughter's getting married to another woman." And just as they get that pitying look in their eye I say, "She's a brain surgeon." and it just blows their mind.

CHARLOTTE. She's not a brain surgeon, mom.

LUCINDA. Doesn't matter.

> (**LUCINDA** *lights a cigarette.*)

HOWARD. Seriously? At lunch? At the table?

LUCINDA. You betcha. Over strawberries.

> *(beat)*

JONNY. It feels so good to be eating a meal with y'all. I can't believe how long it's been.

CHARLOTTE. Jonny and I haven't seen each other for almost a year. Except on Skype. But it's not the same as in the flesh.

> *(She kisses **JONNY** on the cheek, squeezes his arm, something.)*

HOWARD. So what's going on with your mom's house, Jonny?

JONNY. We're closing tomorrow.

HOWARD. Nice people, my new neighbors?

JONNY. I think so. Husband. Wife. Couple of kids.

LUCINDA. End of an era, huh?

JONNY. Especially for my family. That house belonged to my great-great-great-grandfather. But it's been five years since my mom passed and I never come back here so... I cut the cord. *(beat)* I really love California.

CHARLOTTE. Jonny and I have a plan. We'll come back here, once a year –

HOWARD. More than that I hope.

CHARLOTTE. Once a year together, no partners, no spouses, just us. At the fair.

JONNY. I'll watch her ride the roller coaster.

> *(pause)*

HOWARD. *(to* **JONNY***)* So how's the teaching going?

JONNY. I'm taking a break, actually. I've been working on a book this past year, and with the sale of the house and the advance I got –

HOWARD. Advance on the house?

JONNY. Advance on the book.

HOWARD. It's being published? *(beat)* That's great. What is it? Something academic?

JONNY. No, I guess it's fiction.

HOWARD. *(disconcerted)* Really?

JONNY. Yes.

CHARLOTTE. It's called *Letters I Never Wrote My Mother* and it's beautiful.

JONNY. It's kind of a memoir.

HOWARD. Which is it? Fiction or memoir? They're extremely different.

JONNY. Well…it's like…it's what I *wish* had happened. I don't know. It's kind of a new genre. Maybe.

HOWARD. Oh.

LUCINDA. They gave you an advance? People must be pretty excited about it.

CHARLOTTE. He gets all tense talking about it. If you want to know any more, Google him. Or wait until he does all the morning talk shows.

JONNY. It's not going to be big like that.

CHARLOTTE. It might be. They think it might be.

LUCINDA. How's your new one coming, Howard? People excited about it?

HOWARD. Fuck you.

CHARLOTTE. Guys!

HOWARD. People are excited about it. I also got an advance. Carol and I are talking about taking a trip with it. Around the world.

LUCINDA. You hate to travel.

HOWARD. Not with her.

CHARLOTTE. You promised we could eat together as a family and be civil.

(Pause. **LUCINDA** *does her hypnosis inhalation thing.)*

JONNY. You do that *and* smoke?

LUCINDA. And drink.

> *(She takes a sip of wine.)*

HOWARD. Carol's coming to the wedding. Charlotte said it was OK.

CHARLOTTE. *(to* LUCINDA*)* I was going to discuss it with you.

> *(No response from* **LUCINDA**.*)*

JONNY. Thanks for letting me stay at the house tonight.

LUCINDA. You're welcome.

HOWARD. *(at the same time)* You're welcome. *(to* **LUCINDA***)* Not your house anymore.

CHARLOTTE. I'm so frightened you guys are going to ruin the wedding.

LUCINDA. *(to* **CHARLOTTE***)* I am so tired of being your Mammie. "Everything's alright chil', don't you worry about me not having my freedom now, sleep on my titties, I'll sing you a lullaby?"

JONNY. *(not offended, awed)* Jesus.

LUCINDA. *(to* **CHARLOTTE***)* Honey, I can't perform for you any more. Especially now I'm off my meds.

CHARLOTTE. I don't want you to perform for me.

LUCINDA. Yes you do, but I'm done.

HOWARD. You shouldn't *be* off your meds. What kind of therapist are you seeing?

LUCINDA. One who explained I wasn't unhappy because I had a chemical imbalance. I was unhappy because I was married to you!

HOWARD. *(violently)* Behave! She's getting married and you will behave! You want to hate me, you want to blame me –

LUCINDA. He plays the victim. But the truth is he fell out of love with me years ago and was too chicken to admit it.

HOWARD. I would have toughed it out.

LUCINDA. There is nothing successful about an unhappy marriage, you idiot.

HOWARD. There is! Kept promises and character and loyalty –

LUCINDA. You are happier because I left! You are happier with this mouse Carol because I left!

HOWARD. That is not true.

LUCINDA. Do you fuck her?

> (JONNY *and* CHARLOTTE *make a silent joint decision to leave. They get up.*)

He wouldn't fuck me! You two know how important sex is! Well he stopped making love to me!

HOWARD. Behave.

LUCINDA. It was perfunctory! It was the service given by the teenager at the gas tank. Quick and jabby. A summer job he had to do. Howard we are approaching old age! I intend to enjoy my twilight making love!

HOWARD. Can't you keep your emotions in check long enough for us all to have lunch? She's in from D.C. once every six months. Can you not make it so that she never wants to come home? Please?

> (HOWARD *grabs some plates and heads back to the house, containing his emotions. A beat.* CHARLOTTE *runs after him.*)

LUCINDA. Sorry about that, Jonny.

JONNY. I've been in therapy too, over the last few years. It's life-changing, huh?

LUCINDA. Literally.

JONNY. I'm sorry this is happening to you, Lula.

> (LUCINDA *takes his hand across the table.*)

LUCINDA. Jonny. This whole gay marriage thing is very exciting and God bless. But you want my advice? Don't do it.

> (LUCINDA *studies* JONNY'*s hand.*)

JONNY. You reading my fortune?

LUCINDA. My Daddy was a real asshole but he was so great when I was a little girl and I didn't know he was an asshole, you know? I'd rub the knuckles of his right hand while he was driving. And we'd play Hank Williams because I was the only one of my sisters that liked Hank Williams and he loved me for it. Honestly, I don't know if I really liked Hank Williams or if I just wanted him to love me a little bit more than my sisters. Sometimes I think I was testing his love when I introduced him to Howard. I knew he'd hate him, I knew it. But I wanted unconditional love, you know. Not from Howard. From my dad. And when I saw I didn't have it…when he made threats about disinheriting me, marrying a kike…that sent me right down the aisle.

JONNY. *(gently)* You got a beautiful daughter out of it.

LUCINDA. But she's always been a Daddy's girl.

JONNY. Supply and demand. He was always holed up writing.

LUCINDA. Will you do me a favor, Jonny? Dance with me at her wedding? There's nothing worse than being at a wedding and having no one to dance with.

JONNY. Fine. But stand forewarned. I am a terrible dancer.

LUCINDA. We'll just do the slow ones. They're easy. Just got to hold me and sway.

Scene Two

(The family living room, the next afternoon. **HOWARD**, *very agitated, is reading something on his laptop.)*

HOWARD. *(yelling)* Jonny! Jonny get down here!

(Furious, he paces until **JONNY** *enters.)*

JONNY. What's up?

HOWARD. *(pointing at the computer)* What is that? What the fuck is that?

JONNY. Your laptop.

HOWARD. What's *on* the laptop.

*(***JONNY*** *goes over to the laptop and starts reading. He's flustered.)*

JONNY. I don't know how this got here.

HOWARD. Is that the problem? Or is the problem that it *exists?*

JONNY. How did you even find it?

HOWARD. I Googled your name to find out about your fucking book deal.

JONNY. This is something I wrote a very long time ago. I didn't even know it was online. I apologize.

HOWARD. I only read the first paragraph.

JONNY. Good.

HOWARD. Now they want a credit card number. Why should I pay? You're right here in my house. You can tell me face to face why, as you state in your first paragraph, my novels are case studies of casual sexism, racism and homophobia?

(pause)

JONNY. I was going to interview you.

HOWARD. Oh yes! Truffaut. Hitchcock. That was a lot of smoke you blew up my ass.

JONNY. You weren't available. Remember?

HOWARD. So you libeled me? Does Charlotte know about this?

JONNY. No.

(**HOWARD** *Googles something on the laptop.*)

It was just a paper. My professor sent it to the world's most obscure journal.

HOWARD. Great! You Google *my* name and this comes up!

JONNY. Sorry.

HOWARD. How the fuck have I offended you? What did I ever do except write books and love my beautiful gay daughter? Except believe she could be the first female president because there should be a woman president. I have *always* thought women are better than men! And by the way, I have always loved homosexuals! My agent is a homosexual! Without homosexuals the world would be less beautiful! I know that, I get that, I'm one of the good guys! You have offended me. Very, very intensely offended me. That's personal. Now let's get legal. This is slander. I want it off the internet.

JONNY. That's fine, that's great, I told you, it was never meant to be published. I just wrote it really fast, my professor thought it was really good...

HOWARD. I give a lot of money to that school, what professor, what's his name?

JONNY. It was a she.

HOWARD. Of course it was.

JONNY. *(cold)* She was black too. Does that make her even more suspect?

(beat)

HOWARD. You think I'm a racist?

JONNY. It's not slander.

HOWARD. So you stand by this?

JONNY. It's a critical analysis. Authors attract critics. That's legitimate

HOWARD. Fine. Justify your position. Clarify your position.

JONNY. It is *very* clear on the page. In your twenty-nine books there are forty-two homosexual characters. Thirty-eight are what I call underworld figures. Of the shadows and the streets. Criminal.

HOWARD. It's detective fiction, Jonny. Lots of criminals in it.

JONNY. You objectify women constantly. The first sentence in your ninth book is, "Her seventeen year old breasts looked like miniature upside down pie crusts before they'd been baked."

HOWARD. Should I not describe breasts? Is it sexist to acknowledge that breasts exist and to ninety percent of the male population they are phenomenal!

JONNY. Of the one hundred and eight victims in your novel eighty-three are women.

HOWARD. You can't interpret literature with math.

JONNY. Out of all your female murder victims, want to know how many are found naked? All but two.

HOWARD. *(beat)* You know these stats pretty well for a paper you wrote a long time ago.

JONNY. The paper became a part of a lecture. Let's talk about race. Out of your sixteen characters of color that have a significant plot function across your work, want to know how many can dance? All of them!

HOWARD. I have read all of James Baldwin. You may have heard of him. He's a black, gay American canonical novelist. You know what he writes about a lot? How well black people dance! How well they fuck! So fuck you! You want to write about prejudice! Write about your mother! Write about her understanding of good and evil! But obscure little journals don't want to attack black women, they've got it out for straight white men, such an easy target for the academy, well I'm sick of it! You want to rebuild the world in your own fucking image then build it! Don't throw stones at my world, I did the best I could. *(beat)* Jesus, kid. You have been treated like a member of this family your whole life and you call me prejudiced?

JONNY. You never treated me like a member of your family.

HOWARD. You're kidding.

JONNY. I *never* felt welcome. Not when you were in the room. I cut my knee. Lucinda gave me a band-aid. "Thank you, Lula," I said, because that's all I'd heard anybody call her. You said, "Actually, Jonny, Lula is a family name."

HOWARD. I have no memory of that.

JONNY. Charlotte brought home a guy she was dating. I came for dinner, you turned to him and you said, "You make a good point, son." You have *never* called me son.

HOWARD. That must be because I'm a sexist, homophobic racist.

JONNY. You called him "son." A tall, white, football-playing stranger.

HOWARD. You're right –

JONNY. Well that's a first in this house.

HOWARD. I had a problem with you. And it had nothing to do with the color of your skin or what you like to do with your dick. My problem is that you are tricky. You never could look anyone in the eye and shake their hand and convey any sense that you were an honest and straightforward individual. That football player walked into the room and right away you could tell he had a sense of himself and I respected that.

JONNY. I was a messed up kid. I didn't know who I was.

HOWARD. That shit may fly with Charlotte, it doesn't work on me. You knew who you were. You were scared of it.

JONNY. Of course I was scared of it! I read your books! I read every book you ever wrote! And so did Charlotte! How did you describe the lesbian in *Snow on Peachtree Street*? Oh, yes. Cursed. No wonder Charlotte cut her wrists.

(*A moment for this to land. Then* **HOWARD** *lunges for* **JONNY**.)

HOWARD. (*to* **JONNY**) You take that back! You take that back!

(They fight. JONNY's stronger but HOWARD is angrier so they are evenly matched.)

(Eventually LUCINDA and CHARLOTTE enter. They carry garment bags containing wedding dresses.)

LUCINDA. Wow!

CHARLOTTE. What the fuck?

(JONNY has HOWARD pinned.)

JONNY. If I let you go, will you stop?

HOWARD. Yes.

CHARLOTTE. What happened?

(JONNY lets HOWARD go. HOWARD lunges again and gets JONNY in a headlock.)

HOWARD. Take it back, take it back!

CHARLOTTE. *(at the same time)* Stop it! Stop it! Stop it!

(JONNY is starting to choke.)

Dad!

(Frightened and shocked, HOWARD releases JONNY, then leaves the room. A beat.)

LUCINDA. Ice.

(She exits. Pause.)

JONNY. There's something I need to tell you. And it's going to upset you. But you will get over it.

CHARLOTTE. *(a little scared)* I guess it upset my dad.

JONNY. *(a joke)* Yeah, he's a little worked up.

CHARLOTTE. *(not laughing)* What did you do?

JONNY. Before I tell, I just want to remind you of something. Your dad's books are a little racist, aren't they? And a little sexist. We've discussed this. Words for snow, remember?

CHARLOTTE. Did you say something nasty to him about his books?

JONNY. There's this class I taught. Teach. On popular fiction.

CHARLOTTE. About my dad?

JONNY. He's part of it. A big part of it.

CHARLOTTE. How long have you been doing that?

JONNY. A year. *(beat)* A couple of years.

> *(pause)*

CHARLOTTE. Oh shit. *(beat)* Are we an illusion?

Scene Three

(The Living Room. Day. Bright. **CHARLOTTE**
is sitting, a laptop open. We hear **JONNY**'s *voice
through the computer. Skype. Maybe we also see real*
JONNY. *But crucial to keep the sense of distance
and connections easily broken.* **CHARLOTTE** *is
cold.)*

JONNY. You're overreacting.

CHARLOTTE. Wrong.

JONNY. I've taken the article down. I've apologized.

CHARLOTTE. I don't want you there. It would upset me. It
would upset my dad.

JONNY. I always looked up to your dad. Because he was a
real writer and I wanted to be one too. Secretly

CHARLOTTE. Of course. Secrets are your favorite thing.

JONNY. *(ignoring this)* And then I read his books. And I
couldn't stop reading them. Even though they made
me feel bad about myself. And I thought they might
have made you feel that way too.

CHARLOTTE. In *real* life, not in books, in real life my father
paid for camp and taught you fractions.

JONNY. If I had understood then that coming over to play
came with so many strings attached I would have stayed
home!

CHARLOTTE. Not strings. Loyalty.

JONNY. No, I'm being accused of biting the hand that
feeds me. Guess what? I am not a dog.

CHARLOTTE. I let you share my family. You didn't even let
me say goodbye to your mother.

JONNY. You're just like your dad, you know that? You're
so fucking controlling. Well guess what? I'm a grown
up independent man and if I want to stand up and
say it like it is to a bunch of kids so that they don't
have to grow up as scared as I did, and you should be
supporting me, and happy for me, and proud of me,

and if you can't be those things… *(He stops himself.)* But I'm also your best man and I love you.

CHARLOTTE. I don't know who you are. I want you to stop calling me. I want you to stop emailing. I want you to go away. *(beat)* Okay?

> (**HOWARD** *enters, in his dressing gown. He guesses she's talking to* **JONNY** *and freezes for a moment.* **HOWARD** *has aged a thousand years since the fight with* **JONNY**.)

JONNY. No that is not okay.

> (**CHARLOTTE** *closes her laptop. No more* **JONNY**.)

CHARLOTTE. *(brightly, to* HOWARD*)* You want some coffee?

HOWARD. I'll get it. You want some more?

> *(He heads to the kitchen – but before he goes:)*

Was that Jonny?

CHARLOTTE. That was the last of Jonny.

HOWARD. You guys have been friends a long time. I wouldn't want to be responsible –

CHARLOTTE. You're not.

> (**CHARLOTTE** *busies herself with something.* **HOWARD** *lingers.*)

HOWARD. Charlotte, I just uh. You know, I – Whatever I did, if I did something, I just want you to know how deeply, deeply, sorry I am. I just write. I never think about… I never considered…

CHARLOTTE. *(not looking up)* I barely read your books. Jonny's the one obsessed with them.

> *(pause)*

HOWARD. You really don't want him at the wedding?

CHARLOTTE. No, because I've met someone for real now.

HOWARD. Who'll be your best man?

CHARLOTTE. I was going to ask you.

(**CHARLOTTE**'s *cell phone starts to ring. She turns it off.*)

CHARLOTTE. And mom can give me away.

(**HOWARD** *nods, uncertain.*)

Scene Four

(A room at the Swallow's Lodge, with all the beige and tapestry that implies.)

(CHARLOTTE and LUCINDA are on the bed, clothed except for naked feet. Their toes are spread out by brightly colored foam separators, their toenail polish is drying. Pedicure accoutrements are on the bed.)

(CHARLOTTE is tense.)

LUCINDA. Night before *my* wedding I got high as a kite.

CHARLOTTE. Well I'm sober, so.

LUCINDA. From what Martha told me, she was the *real* alcoholic. Bottle of vodka, 10 a.m.

CHARLOTTE. Let's change the subject.

LUCINDA. I joined the Peace Corps.

CHARLOTTE. You did? *(beat)* Isn't that for teenagers?

LUCINDA. Apparently my age is an advantage. A few weeks after you get back from your honeymoon I'll be leaving town for a while.

CHARLOTTE. Congratulations.

LUCINDA. I thank you.

> *(beat)*

CHARLOTTE. I thought now that you're footloose and fancy free you might come up to D.C. and spend some time with us. We're talking about having a baby, you know. At some point.

LUCINDA. And at some point I'll be there. I promise you.

> *(pause)*

The tux looks so sharp on you.

CHARLOTTE. Really?

LUCINDA. I get it now. It's very rock star.

CHARLOTTE. It's just a costume anyway. The whole thing is just costumes.

LUCINDA. Honey, do you not like the tux?

CHARLOTTE. I like it fine.

LUCINDA. Honey it's your wedding! You have to like the dress! Or the pant suit!

CHARLOTTE. I like it more than anything else I found.

LUCINDA. Oh honey, no! You have to feel beautiful on your wedding day.

CHARLOTTE. Martha's beautiful.

LUCINDA. I don't give a shit about Martha! I give a shit about you. Listen, I think the tux looks great but if you're not happy we will drive to a mall right now and I swear we will find something.

CHARLOTTE. I do like it. I do. I'm just nervous.

LUCINDA. There's nothing to be nervous about. You can always get divorced.

CHARLOTTE. I wish your sisters *weren't* coming. You should have checked with me before saying yes.

LUCINDA. I was excited they changed their mind.

CHARLOTTE. Everyone in the world is coming. Except Jonny.

(**LUCINDA** *decides not to comment on that.*)

CHARLOTTE. Nothing's how it was supposed to be. Nothing. You and Dad aren't together. I'm marrying a woman. The whole thing's just going to look weird.

LUCINDA. Honey, weird is good. I promise you. You think it didn't look weird when God created the world? There was all that nothingness and then…what the fuck is all of that? Weird is life. Take a close look at a fish. Weird.

(*beat*)

CHARLOTTE. You said you didn't want to perform for me, remember?

LUCINDA. Yes.

CHARLOTTE. So, I know you and Dad are disappointed that I'm not marrying a guy.

LUCINDA. I can't imagine a guy in the world as special as Martha.

CHARLOTTE. Dad's disappointed. He's being really big about it, but he wanted me to marry that football player. Or that movie star.

LUCINDA. Dad was going to be disappointed in whoever you married. He is a Jew. There is never *not* a problem.

(pause)

CHARLOTTE. Carol *is* a mouse. I wish she wasn't coming to the wedding.

LUCINDA. You're going to have such a good time tomorrow you won't even know she's there.

CHARLOTTE. Are you seeing anyone?

LUCINDA. Unlike your dad, I feel no need for companionship. Between now and forever all I want are short, sharp bursts of life.

CHARLOTTE. What does that mean?

LUCINDA. I'm seeing several people.

CHARLOTTE. *(taking this in)* Do you meet them online?

LUCINDA. Hell no, I do it the old fashioned way. Bars and supermarkets. Making up for lost time. I'm fifty years old. I'm not ready to put my orgasm in a drawer. I wasn't ready when I was thirty-five either.

(beat)

CHARLOTTE. Did you guys really not have sex for fifteen years?

LUCINDA. I don't want to tell tales out of school here –

CHARLOTTE. Good, that's best.

LUCINDA. But the very last time we did it, August fourth, seven summers ago, he stopped in the middle because he was trying to remember a telephone number. *(beat)* It's funny but it's not funny.

CHARLOTTE. *(beat)* I'm torn between wanting more details and wanting a more significant mother-daughter boundary.

LUCINDA. I know, right? It's so hard to know when to be mother and daughter and when to be friends. I'll follow your lead.

CHARLOTTE. Was Dad just not *capable?*

LUCINDA. Don't marry a writer, honey. All that time alone, with a computer. I'd check his browser history. Oh, he was capable.

> *(beat)*

CHARLOTTE. I want us to be friends.

> *(beat)*

LUCINDA. Walking through that house after you left for college, you know what I kept thinking about? My sister Stephanie's cat. And how it died. It died a month after she went to college. And it was odd because it was in perfect health, the prime of life. Nobody knew what the hell happened. But I knew. That cat died because no one in that house gave a damn about it after my sister had gone. You were gone. Your father was writing. And I could not stop thinking about that dead cat.

CHARLOTTE. You sure it wasn't something it ate.

LUCINDA. It was an absence of love.

CHARLOTTE. But Dad does love you. He still loves you.

LUCINDA. But he's not *in* love with me. He's not in love with Carol either. He just likes someone waiting for him. In the other room.

CHARLOTTE. You stayed so long because of me, didn't you?

LUCINDA. I almost left one time. Well you know all about that.

CHARLOTTE. Do I? No I don't. What?

> **(LUCINDA** *looks at her confused.)*

When did you almost leave?

LUCINDA. That night. That night you…

CHARLOTTE. Oh.

LUCINDA. You knew that. That was why… You heard us. Fighting about me leaving.

CHARLOTTE. I don't remember.

LUCINDA. The psychiatrist said you knew I was leaving and you freaked out. He blamed me.

CHARLOTTE. I didn't know that. We drove home in silence. We never talk about this.

LUCINDA. We're discussing it now.

CHARLOTTE. I don't want to. It's the night before my wedding.

LUCINDA. I apologize.

CHARLOTTE. I don't even know how we got onto this.

LUCINDA. We eliminated a boundary.

CHARLOTTE. Oh right.

LUCINDA. Let's put it right back up.

CHARLOTTE. You should not have blamed yourself. He should not have blamed you. I didn't say anything like that. I didn't say hardly anything at all. You must have told him you were fighting. He asked me if that was why. I said yes. It was just easier. I wanted to get out of there. Shit!

> *(**CHARLOTTE** has messed up the drying nails on one of her feet.)*

LUCINDA. I'll take care of it.

> *(She takes **CHARLOTTE**'s foot in her lap and re-beautifies the nail.)*

I love that your nail polish is your something blue. *(no response)* We got too serious didn't we, and we shouldn't have. That's my fault. *(beat)* When you were a little girl and you got sad do you remember what I'd do?

CHARLOTTE. *(grim)* Don't do it.

> *(**LUCINDA** lunges at **CHARLOTTE**.)*

LUCINDA. Tickle tickle tickle!

(She tickles **CHARLOTTE** *and* **CHARLOTTE** *can't help laughing. The tickle-tussle becomes a very tight hug.)*

CHARLOTTE. Now you've messed up both our nails.

LUCINDA. Let's start again.

(She takes **CHARLOTTE**'*s foot, and removes all the nail polish. She does not look up as:)*

CHARLOTTE. I told Whitney I was in love with Jasmine. But that was dumb because Whitney told Ashley and Kayla. And Jasmine. And they came and found me in the bathroom at recess. And they asked me about it. "I never said I was in *love* with Jasmine. I said I loved her." That's what I said, quick as a flash. And I saw them consider this little word "in" and whether or not it made a difference. And I was thinking about it too, was leaving out that one word going to save me? And then Kayla said, "If you didn't say it then why are you about to cry? There are tears in your eyes." I said, "No, there's not." But there were. And they were about to spill out. Then Kayla said, "Blink." And the three of them were just staring, waiting. So I blinked. And somehow the lid of my eye pushed back the tears. Nothing ran down my face. I thought God saved me. Now I have to change. That night I decided to become an Orthodox Jew and slept like a baby. The next morning I walked to the bathroom and cut my wrists. It had nothing to do with you and Dad fighting. It had to do with me realizing there was a major problem with the way I fell in love.

(Pause. Really long.)

LUCINDA. *(firmly)* Well there is no way you could have handled a divorce. Not with all that going on.

CHARLOTTE. No one knows that story except Martha.

LUCINDA. Not Jonny?

CHARLOTTE. Jonny was the only kid at school who never asked me why. That was one of the things I liked about him.

(knock at the door)

LUCINDA. *(calling out)* It's open!

*(**HOWARD** enters. He's carrying a big box.)*

HOWARD. Surprise! *(to **LUCINDA**)* You could have stayed at the house.

CHARLOTTE. She thinks this is Bohemian.

LUCINDA. *(at the same time)* This is Bohemian. You're intruding.

HOWARD. I know, but I did a thing and I didn't know if it would come off but it has. Maybe. *(to **CHARLOTTE**)* I know you don't love the tux. And although I absolutely think it's great if you want to wear a tux I have been on a hunt this last month and the hunt has come to an end. *(He hands her the box.)* You don't have to like it, you don't have to wear it. But this was your mother's wedding dress. Which, in an attempt to send a message to me, not caring how it affected her only child, she sold on eBay to a woman in Oregon. Said woman, since purchasing the damn dress, now lives off the grid and it was quite a challenge to track down her earthship. However, I don't write detective fiction for nothing. I succeeded. I bought back the dress at twice the price, please note how this woman professes to live outside the capitalist system but in fact is an exemplar of said system. The dress arrived, by FedEx an hour ago. And if you want to wear it a lady will come by the house and do alterations in the morning. You're welcome.

LUCINDA. *(to **HOWARD**)* I remember you. Didn't we fall in love?

HOWARD. *(to **CHARLOTTE**)* You don't have to wear it honey. It's just another option. But it will look great. It looked great on Bob Dylan over there.

*(He means **LUCINDA**.)*

CHARLOTTE. You don't think two dresses will look weird?

HOWARD. No!

LUCINDA. *(at the same time)* You need to get over that! Go try it on.

CHARLOTTE. I make no promises.

LUCINDA. Do what you want, we love the tux.

> (**CHARLOTTE** *exits to the bathroom.*)

God bless you, I hate that fucking tux. Although of course, if she was transgendered, nothing but support. Jesus, having kids is exhausting.

HOWARD. *(through the bathroom door, to* **CHARLOTTE***)* Listen, Jonny came by the house. *(beat)* He's in town. He's in town specifically in case you change your mind.

> *(pause)*

LUCINDA. You wouldn't be this mad at him if you didn't love him, honey. Hate and love are totally connected.

HOWARD. *(to* **LUCINDA***)* Really? Tell it to the Nazis. *(to* **CHARLOTTE***)* You're not keeping Jonny away on my account I hope. Because I have forgiven him. He opened my eyes in a way. *(to* **LUCINDA***)* Did she tell you? I'm pitching a new series to my publishers. Lead character. Black lesbian. A former prostitute. My agent loves it. And so does HBO.

> (**HOWARD** *checks* **CHARLOTTE***'s out of earshot.*)

Jonny changed the title of his book from *Letters I Never Wrote My Mother* to *Letters I Never Wrote*. There's four letters to me in there. He gave them to me.

LUCINDA. And?

HOWARD. They're very moving. You know he never knew his biological father and sometimes he'd pretend it was me. But it was complicated too because I was white and he didn't want a white father and also he was kind of attracted to me.

LUCINDA. He was *not*.

HOWARD. It's implied. There's a whole section about him wanting me to muss his hair and it's deliberately and interestingly quasi-sexual.

LUCINDA. Says you.

HOWARD. He had powerful emotions surrounding me. There's a whole section where he describes beating me, almost to death. It's great. He really goes there. I had a son. I had a son this whole time.

LUCINDA. Howard, he's not *actually* your son.

HOWARD. Of *course* he was a little off. He's a writer. Writers are *off.* I am *off.*

LUCINDA. That's one word for it.

HOWARD. He wrote letters to Charlotte. Said he mailed them. *(loud)* Did you get Jonny's letters honey?

LUCINDA. She wants to be focused on Martha. And that's quite right.

HOWARD. A wedding is let bygones be bygones time. Even your sisters have figured that out.

LUCINDA. Listen, it breaks my heart. Everything seemed right with the world when I watched those two kids play under the tree. I'd turn off the radio so I could hear them laugh. They were beautiful. But they were kids.

HOWARD. Carol and I aren't really going around the world you know. I mean, she wants to but…

LUCINDA. You'd rather be working.

(**HOWARD** *nods.*)

HOWARD. Maybe we'll take a short trip. I don't know.

CHARLOTTE. *(from the bathroom)* Mom, can you come in and button me up?

HOWARD. *(to* **CHARLOTTE,** *excited)* How's it look?

LUCINDA. I'm going to see her in that dress and cry like a baby.

HOWARD. Me too. *(beat)* See? I did something right.

(**LUCINDA** *gives him a hard kiss on the lips.*)

LUCINDA. We did a lot of things right.

(**LUCINDA** *enters the bathroom.*)

(from the bathroom) Howard get in here! Get in here and see how beautiful she looks!

Scene Five

(Under the tree. Night. At the front of the house, the wedding. Somewhere else, colored lights. Somewhere else laughter. Somewhere else music. Here, mostly darkness. Quiet.)

(HOWARD leads CHARLOTTE by the hand. She's in her wedding dress, laughing.)

CHARLOTTE. What? What's so important? I'm supposed to be mingling...

HOWARD. I have something for you.

CHARLOTTE. I didn't know you could be so happy! I didn't know!

(She hugs her father.)

HOWARD. Listen, listen. I want this to be a perfect day.

CHARLOTTE. It has been!

HOWARD. I don't want you to look back and feel like something was missing.

CHARLOTTE. Like what?

HOWARD. Jonny.

(JONNY appears from the shadows. He's in a suit.)

JONNY. Yes?

HOWARD. No, I wasn't cueing you, I was saying you were what was missing.

JONNY. *(worried)* Sorry.

CHARLOTTE. Why is he here?

HOWARD. No you listen to me. You hear me out. You love this young man – yes you do. You *do.* My dad's out there. And I'll tell you something, I hate my father. I *hate* him. But I love him. And I needed him to come tonight. There are going to be photos. This is forever. *I'm* the one Jonny wrote about. I have forgiven him. He has forgiven me for nearly choking him to death. In fact we're quite close now.

(**JONNY** *nods. The two men put their arms around each other's shoulders, demonstratively.*)

HOWARD. I would like to dance with the closest thing I have to a son at your wedding.

CHARLOTTE. Too bad.

(**CHARLOTTE** *starts to exit,* **JONNY** *runs after, grabs her hand.*)

JONNY. Would you just hear me out? You don't answer my calls, you don't write back to my emails.

CHARLOTTE. I don't read them. I have to get back. I've left Martha talking to a horrific aunt I never met.

(**HOWARD** *discreetly exits.*)

JONNY. Stephanie? You did meet her once. There was a very awkward tea years ago. You forced me to attend.

CHARLOTTE. It's great that you and my dad are best buds now, but I gotta go.

JONNY. I don't give a shit about your dad. I give a shit about you.

CHARLOTTE. Our whole thing, it was a joke, it was an act. I look back at us, I feel so sad. Two frightened little kids hiding away from other people and pretending to be soul mates because they thought they needed each other. Because they had to hide. *(beat)* I didn't *understand* I could have a wedding. I never knew I could have a life partner, one that I really wanted. One that I loved completely. One that wouldn't cower in the corner when I took my clothes off.

JONNY. Great. Now you know. You still need friends. We can't be friends until you forgive me.

CHARLOTTE. Look, I forgave you for letting me go through all that coming-out *shit* alone when we could have gone through it together.

JONNY. *(off her tone)* See I don't think you really did.

CHARLOTTE. Because, you're a fucking coward! I came out to my parents, you waited until your mother was dead.

JONNY. And do you have any idea how much I regret that? I don't know that. I haven't had that yet. She never knew who I was! You know that you're loved unconditionally.

(*JONNY's voice breaks. It looks like she's about to see him cry for a second time.*)

CHARLOTTE. I don't trust you any more. You're a locked-up filing cabinet and you swear there's nothing important inside and then out of nowhere you'll pull out some incredibly important document and say, "Oh I'm sorry. This was in here all along, but it doesn't mean anything." But it does mean something. What you keep inside is who you fucking are and you never told me what was inside. You barely let me inside your house!

JONNY. Charlotte, I've been lying my entire life. To everyone! I'm trying to get better. You're walking away while I'm trying to get better? I do love you completely. If we were straight I'd kiss you now, to make you believe me. But we're not so I don't have that option. So I've only got words. And I don't know how to arrange the alphabet the right way to make you believe me.

CHARLOTTE. I have to get back to Martha.

JONNY. Pah!

(*JONNY has executed a dance move. I don't know if it's Liza doing Fosse or Travolta in* Saturday Night Live *but it is a bold gesture.* **CHARLOTTE** *stares. She loves him.*)

CHARLOTTE. What is that?

JONNY. That is dance.

(*And then, as fast as he can,* **JONNY** *undresses.* **CHARLOTTE** *continues to stare.*)

CHARLOTTE. And what is this?

JONNY. This is only fair.

CHARLOTTE. I have to go. Martha –

JONNY. Martha will be fine. She's amazing, remember? You couldn't find a better partner, blah blah blah. She's the best. She's Jewish. She's a doctor. She can dance. But we're *us*, remember?

(He's down to his underwear.)

CHARLOTTE. Don't.

JONNY. I understand that what I'm about to show you will repel you. But you showed me yours.

(He takes off his underpants.)

This is me. And this is me dancing.

(He dances for her. She stares, softening.)

Everyone assumes homosexuals can dance too. I really labor under a tremendous amount of stereotypes and expectations.

*(**HOWARD'S FATHER** enters under the tree. At first he doesn't see them. They see him and freeze. He lights a cigarette, turns and sees **CHARLOTTE** and naked **JONNY**. The cigarette falls from his lips. Pause.)*

CHARLOTTE. Grandpa, I don't think you ever met my friend, Jonny. *(clarifying the situation)* Nothing's going on here. He's a homosexual.

*(**HOWARD'S FATHER** beats a hasty retreat. **CHARLOTTE** and **JONNY** look at each other.)*

Maybe you should…

JONNY. Yeah.

*(**JONNY** puts on his underpants.)*

CHARLOTTE. You're here.

JONNY. Yeah…

(They move towards each other. They hug. At the front of the house where the wedding guests we never see are, muffled by the distance, a song starts. A classic.**)

The whole day I wanted to gatecrash, like this was a romantic comedy.

**See Music Use Note on Copyright Page (page 3).

CHARLOTTE. *(a wail)* I wanted to ask you if I should have worn the dress or the tux. And you missed the ceremony and we can never get that back.

JONNY. I was in my mom's yard. I wore a suit. I stood up. I was silent. *(beat)* I was present.

> *(They dance.)*

CHARLOTTE. Martha can lead. I told her I hated dancing and normally she lets me alone but one time, early on, she just swooped in while I was in the middle of a conversation and she held me just so and somehow she danced me right across the room. And my feet knew what they were doing. And I couldn't stop laughing.

JONNY. Will's obsessed with roller coasters.

CHARLOTTE. You're still with Will…

JONNY. I went on one with him. Afterwards I threw up, but I did.

> **(HOWARD** *and* **LUCINDA** *rush out.)*

HOWARD. What the hell's happening out here?

LUCINDA. Jonny, put your clothes back on!

> **(CHARLOTTE** *and* **JONNY** *keep swaying.)*

HOWARD. That is so beautiful.

> *(He moves to join them.)*

LUCINDA. Howard, leave them be. Jeez-Louise…

> **(HOWARD** *is in the circle.)*

JONNY. *(to* **HOWARD***)* Oh. Hello.

HOWARD. Come join us, Lula. The night is young, the moon is full –

LUCINDA. The wedding is that way. And we are not being gracious hosts.

> *(But as she's talking,* **HOWARD** *goes to get her. She resists but just a little.)*

HOWARD. And we will not pass this way again.

> **(LUCINDA** *is in the circle.)*

CHARLOTTE. *(to* **LUCINDA***)* And hello to you. Welcome.

> *(A beat. The family becomes a swaying circle. Until:)*

I've got to go. Martha will be pissed. Put on your clothes and come join.

> *(***CHARLOTTE*** *exits.* **JONNY** *hurriedly dresses.)*

HOWARD. I shall go placate my father.

> *(He exits.)*

LUCINDA. This time in three weeks I'll be in Uzbeckistan. *(off* **JONNY***'s look)* I joined the Peace Corps. It wasn't my first choice, but whatever. I'll miss this air.

> *(She looks at* **JONNY** *for a response but he's busy dressing.)*

Time, time, time, time, time. Jesus Christ. I feel so fucking free.

> *(***JONNY** *is close to dressed now. He approaches* **LUCINDA**, *ready to take her back to the wedding. He checks his shirt.)*

JONNY. I hope I didn't get grass stains on this.

LUCINDA. Hey.

JONNY. What?

LUCINDA. Love ya, kid.

> *(***JONNY** *stares at her. He smiles. Abrupt blackout.)*

End of Play